Goblin
Fruit

Goblin Fruit

STORIES

David M C 11/09

DAVID MARSHALL CHAN

To Jee :

Best of luck with your
own writing !!!

David M

CONTEXT BOOKS   NEW YORK

2003

The story "Mystery Boy" makes use of nine short phrases or fragments of dialogue, employed for satire or parody, from *The Mystery of the Chinese Junk* (© 1988, 1960 by Simon & Schuster, Inc.) by "Franklin W. Dixon." Portions of this story first appeared in the 1998/99 "Revisions" theme issue of *Columbia*.

www.contextbooks.com

Book design: Cassandra Pappas
Jacket design: Carol Devine Carson
Typeface: Monotype Baskerville

Context Books
368 Broadway
Suite 314
New York, NY 10013

Library of Congress Cataloging-in-Publication Data
Chan, David Marshall.
  Goblin fruit / David Marshall Chan.
    p. cm.
  ISBN 1-893956-32-6 (alk. paper)
    1. Los Angeles (Calif.)—Fiction. 2. Asian Americans—Fiction. I. Title.
PS3603.H3556 G63 2003
813'.6—dc21   2002010110

9   8   7   6   5   4   3   2   1

Manufactured in the United States of America

We must not look at Goblin men,
We must not buy their fruits;
Who knows upon what soil they fed
Their hungry, thirsty roots?

—CHRISTINA ROSSETTI
Goblin Market

A little voice inside my head
said, "Don't look back,
you can never look back."

—DON HENLEY
The Boys of Summer

Contents

Goblin
Fruit

LOST YEARS

1

Out there on the road we didn't have much to do, so when the orange butterflies first appeared to us they were a welcome distraction. Sometimes their number seemed endless, flying together like a blanket in front of the windshield, blocking our grandfather's view. Whenever we stopped for gas and to use the restroom, Tommy and I traced our names on the dirty windshield, our index fingers afterwards covered with a cake of black dirt and bright-colored sparkles from the wings, what we called butterfly dust.

When we returned from the restroom, we always found our names had disappeared, erased.

The gas station attendants were kept busy that season wiping windshields clean. The truck drivers we encountered—big, bearded men who sometimes scared us, who sometimes gave Tommy and me sticks of gum—

told stories about how the butterflies had been causing trouble for weeks, how some people had even gotten into minor accidents or spilled their cargo.

We learned that every year, thousands of these butterflies flew down together from Canada and traveled along the west coast, devouring patches of milkweed as they moved south towards Mexico. According to the truck drivers old enough to remember, this season was the worst ever, even more terrible than the season six years ago when a big rig crashed and started a twenty-car pile-up, all because of the butterflies.

Six years, I thought, was almost my whole life. It was one half of Tommy's age, and he was five years older than me. Along with our grandparents, we were heading in the direction opposite the butterflies, leaving Los Angeles for Canada, driving north.

To me Canada was still an idea. It meant maple leaves and hockey, a place of safety. In my grandmother's mind Canada meant Vancouver, with its large Chinatown where friends of hers lived, where we might be able to lose ourselves. My grandmother spoke no English, but she wasn't shy about speaking to my grandfather in front of the gas station attendants, telling him to carefully count the change when she suspected the attendant might try to cheat us because we were Chinese.

Grandmother was always scared, always on the lookout for those who meant us harm, and the butterfly swarms only further unnerved her. Since the second day of our journey, when we were still in California, we met them head-on in our green '68 Mustang. I never thought such small, delicate things, with wings that tore like paper, could cause so much trouble, that they could take out large trucks. And years later, after the appearances in court, after all the interviews and judges, the endless circle of new and unwelcoming homes, I would think the same thing about my brother and me, amazed by how the two of us alone could cause so much trouble.

But the trip up north wasn't so bad at times, even though our grandparents seemed constantly on edge. We were always in a hurry, never staying in one place too long, always moving ahead. And driving suddenly into a swarm of butterflies on the road was like getting lost in a hurricane of wings. When grandfather refused to pull over to wait for them to fly past us, he would tell Tommy to reach over and turn on the windshield wipers. That's how we usually sat, Tommy and grandfather up front, my grandmother and me in the back.

Sometimes any orange butterflies flying too close to the wipers got caught and turned green, smeared across the glass. Whenever this happened I would hear grandmother say, under her breath, *Not a good sign.*

Grandmother was always talking about such things, about good luck and signs.

I just looked away.

We all sat quietly until we arrived at the next gas station, or the next motel, or the next coffee shop, where someone would eventually have to clean the stains off the glass.

2

The butterflies we encountered always came upon us unexpectedly. One minute the road was clear, and the next we were in a storm of wings.

The way we ended up living with our grandparents in Los Angeles was like that, too. One day we were with our mother in Chicago, and the next day we were in L.A. One day we were there, and the next day we weren't.

Our mother had a habit of disappearing for days at a time, leaving Tommy and me alone in the apartment, preparing ourselves T.V. dinners, canned soup, hard-boiled eggs, and ramen noodles. Once Tommy got a severe burn on his hand after spilling a pot of boiling water, and once we left the oven on for two days, not realizing it until our mother came back from one of her vacations away from us.

We learned how to not answer the phone when the bill collectors called, how to pretend not to be home when social workers notified by our teachers came knocking on the front door.

Despite her instabilities, the court we went to granted our mother custody of Tommy and me. Despite all his problems, our father still believed he could be a better guardian, and that day in Chicago our father picked us up for one of our visits, but instead of going to a Bears game or to the zoo we went straight to the airport. He put us on a plane, without any luggage or a change of clothes, and handed us some dollar bills to rent a set of headphones on the flight.

When the lights dimmed for the movie we both listened, Tommy with his right ear and me with my left. And when the plane landed our grandparents were there at the airport waiting, and they brought us to an apartment we had never laid eyes on before. We had not seen them for months, and now we knew where they had been, waiting for us.

Leaving Los Angeles was the same—one day we were there, and the next we weren't.

We left suddenly, our grandparents convinced the authorities in Chicago had tracked us down. What furniture they couldn't sell—most of it—was abandoned. The furniture was cheap, all they could afford, but still it hurt—even then I knew—it hurt for my grandparents to simply leave it. I remember their house in Chicago: the kitchen drawers full of used pieces of foil and plastic wrap, the plates from T.V. dinners on the shelves alongside the real china, the chairs with broken legs put back together with duct tape, the paint on the ceilings peeling.

So my brother and I, we knew it was serious when we left Los Angeles. By then Tommy was no longer Tommy—he was Michael. And I was someone different also—I was now M———. We had to remember this when we started our new schools in L.A., but this pretending lasted only a few months before we were told to bring everything home. There wasn't much in my desk—some pencils, erasers, a red notebook, and a few pennies. I did as my grandmother told me and I looked in the dimly-lit coat closet of the classroom for anything I might have forgotten, but it was empty except for the same blue sweater that had been hanging there since the middle of September.

Our time in Los Angeles had passed quickly, more memorable for what we could have done than for what we actually did. Tommy constantly begged to be taken to Hollywood Boulevard, to go to the movie theaters there or to look at the stars on the sidewalk, like the one we saw Lucy and Ethel try to steal on *I Love Lucy*. Our apartment wasn't too far from Hollywood Boulevard, and many nights we were startled awake by the sound of gunfire, sirens, and the roar of low-flying helicopters.

One night Tommy snuck out and wandered along the Boulevard, but he didn't have enough money to get into one of the movie theaters or the Hollywood Wax Museum like he wanted. When he returned I was almost as angry with him as my grandparents. By then even I knew that what was happening to us wasn't a game. I could, at times, even begin to understand that the secret lives we had been taught to live, away from the reach of our mother, were maybe for the best. That Tommy couldn't see this for himself was, for me, most likely the beginning of my contempt for him, which would later grow into years of silence.

My father also became the object of my scorn. During those months in L.A. we'd received periodic calls from him. All that time, he was only a voice on the phone. *I'll be with you soon*, he promised. *When I come I'll be bringing a puppy.*

The plan, I knew, was for us to eventually find a way to live with him, and the reason for being with our grandparents was it made it more difficult for the police to track us. But our father had never been a large part of our lives, and he was becoming only a bad memory, one quickly fading away.

When he called, he'd speak about a new apartment in a better neighborhood, but I knew he was lying; he was always lying. It was obvious we had very little money. I found out from my grandmother that their farmhouse outside Chicago had been sold, lost to us now. I kept asking about it, about what little I could remember. I wanted to know about the things I missed— the books and records and toys we left behind, the things from the farmhouse I liked when I visited, like the old fashioned wind-up record player in grandmother's sewing room that I always thought was called a grandma-phone.

We wouldn't have the money to replace all those things, I knew. Grandmother promised we'd live in a big house one day soon, and how she would open bank accounts in our names so that Tommy and I could buy new cars when we turned eighteen.

But driving up the coast the old car kept stalling; the engine made noises warning that it would soon break down. We ate mostly peanut butter sandwiches, and we were always hungry. We slept in the car if we could find somewhere safe to park, and whenever we checked into a motel, we shared a single room.

At every motel, grandmother burned incense for

good luck. I didn't understand her superstitions, the ways she relieved her fears. I'd open the windows so we wouldn't get in trouble for setting off the fire alarm. At times like those, I would be furious, thinking I was the only one among us with any common sense.

Tommy and I slept in a foldout cot while grandmother and grandfather shared the one bed. At night I could hear everyone breathing as I laid awake in the unfamiliar darkness waiting to fall asleep. I had noticed that my grandparents were usually quiet, and when they spoke they did so only to us kids, and not to each other. Maybe it was this silence between them, I thought, that made it possible for them to stay together for so long. Our own parents were always talking when they were together, and maybe this was their problem.

3

Sometimes it seemed as if we were headed nowhere— our days were a series of stops and starts, stops and starts.

I remember all the cemeteries we passed, each one indistinguishable from all the others along the roads we traveled. Passing by them, I always looked for the mounds of dirt indicating freshly dug graves where the newly dead had been laid to rest.

.   .   .

On the road grandmother always appeared tired and weak. Our travel seemed endless, and in truth, I don't think my grandparents knew for sure what would happen once we reached our destination. At the end of each day we seemed no closer to our goal. Sometimes we drove for just two hours the whole day, spending our time wandering a park or a new city; and sometimes we drove back towards L.A., because grandfather thought following an unusual, unpredictable route made us more difficult to track. When there was a city we liked, we stayed a couple of days, sleeping in the car. I don't remember how long our trip took—back then, time seemed to stop, and the only thing I knew was that we were always moving.

Often I looked out the window at the cars next to us, illuminated by all the headlights on the road, and it seemed like no one was moving at all. Of course this was just a trick of the eye—all the cars were really moving at a similar speed—but it was fun to think we were all just standing still.

One night we drove past a factory and observed thick black smoke gushing out from the roof. At first we thought the factory was on fire, but then we realized that this was the same smoke the factory put out all day long, and we were just viewing it in the dark. The slow movement of the black billows of smoke across the clear, evening sky was beautiful. I wanted to roll down the window to smell it, but grandmother wouldn't let me. It was a mild, still night with no trace of wind. The smoke clouds seemed to hang in the air, suspended.

As we were resting in a public park one day I found a friendly stray cat. It was happy as could be playing in a large JCPenney paper bag we had in the car, and I thought that if we kept her the bag could be her home. I watched the cat clean herself for hours, and my grandparents humored me by letting me take her along with us. The next day, though, we discovered from the cat's behavior that she was probably a bit crazy, so we abandoned her alongside the road. I had not even had enough time to give her a name, but during the one day I had her, I knew I loved her.

The cat's bizarre behavior reminded me of my mother. I understood that, given her problems, she did the best she could with us. And compared to our father, at least she didn't drink and had never been in jail. But with her problems, our mother never held a job for too long, and our time with her in one sense prepared us for the years ahead as we moved from apartment to apartment, bad neighborhood to bad neighborhood, our lives in constant motion.

•   •   •

The apartment we had with our grandparents in Holly-wood was in as bad an area as where we lived in Chicago. I remember on Halloween all the houses with the lights turned off, not offering any candy. If we kept knocking someone might scream out through the door, in a voice both angry and sad, *We have no money!* After that we understood, so we just went on with our masks and near-empty bags to the next house and to the convenience stores on Hollywood Boulevard, where we hoped to score some Snickers. But still, we were mad at being turned away.

Occasionally I would glance out the window and read the names of the roads and cities we were passing, names I knew I would soon forget and never need to know of in the future.

Some cities we drove through like ghosts: we appeared and then we disappeared.

Once on the road a lone man on a motorcycle sped by us and then disappeared around the next curve. As he passed us he glanced my way and caught me staring at him, and he looked me in the eye through his sunglasses and nodded at me. I wanted so much then to trade places with him. As I watched him disappear, I thought to myself, *I wish that were me.*

4

On the road, our grandmother was the most nervous of us all. She knew the danger of what we were doing, and in the car or the motel room she always clutched an old, tattered Chinese Bible and a jewelry box full of good luck charms. I once opened the box to see what was hidden in there, and I found a ring, a bronze bracelet, a pair of silver earrings shaped like half moons, some old coins, a jade Buddha statue, postcards and letters written in Chinese that I couldn't read, and small little cardboard cylinders that contained important-looking documents rolled inside them. Looking at all these old things I realized how many years she had lived; the thought that even with her age our situation still scared her made me more frightened myself.

We were all jittery in the car. Our grandparents' fears rubbed off on us. There were so many things to watch out for—the police, menacing truckers, drunk drivers—so many bad things on the road. Grandfather allowed us to play the radio, but softly.

The stations changed as we headed from city to city. We'd be listening to one station and as we drove further the reception became less clear and more faint until finally it died out altogether and we were left with static or silence.

It was a surprise to realize the stations we listened to couldn't be heard by other people somewhere else, just as my sense of displacement was heightened when we first arrived in L.A. and I discovered that some of the T.V. shows I watched in Chicago were not shown there. I had always assumed before that anywhere in the country someone could turn on the T.V. and see the same thing I was watching at home.

When we first got into the state of Washington, with neither a T.V. nor a home, grandmother's hands were shaking. She made grandfather stop in front of a church because she wanted to go in and pray. He never read the Bible and wouldn't step into any church, so Tommy and I waited outside with him drinking sodas. We sat in front of the church under a large rusted statue of some saint or angel. The inscription on the base of the figure read: WE MOVE TOWARD WHAT WE THINK.

Grandmother came out looking different than when she went in, although she was wearing the same clothes and her hair was still white like before. She appeared calmer. And then it was time to move on.

5

And that was the beginning, the start of the lost years.

I didn't know then of the difficulties in the years to come, nor the fact that one day it would all end and my life would come crashing down, and then I would legally and in every other sense be the only person left to pick it up, to love it and save it, to be in charge of it. But back then the journey we were on seemed at times like some fantastic story out of a picture book, one where all the problems would be fixed—all the worries gone, conflicts resolved, scars healed—before I could get to the words THE END.

In Seattle during the last days of the trip, our sightings of the butterflies became rarer. It was drizzling and foggy, the roads dark and wet, and I wondered where it was that butterflies went to get out of the rain. That image of Seattle was one I kept in my mind and saved for the future, and years later the idea of the weather in Seattle being perpetually bad seemed to me to be not far from the truth.

There was so much to be careful of in those years, so much both good and bad, like the truckers who we could trust and those who tried to run us off the road and told us to *go back home*. I wished we had one to return to, and not our life of motels and new keys, gas station restrooms, the blur of new faces and voices and road signs, and the ever-shifting, ever-changing landscape and rooms that we left before they ever became familiar.

That time on the run was full of confusion, and the strangeness of the road. It was a year marked by the weirdness and the beauty of the butterflies, flying in and out of our lives, then disappearing with the rains.

It was a time when my grandfather could be heard humming along to a song on the radio, a map of Canada we bought in a Seattle gas station in his lap, when I would suddenly fly hard against the side of the car as he recklessly made a sharp turn because of something he thought he saw in the rear view mirror. And before I can begin dreaming of a life with a familiar bed and a constant phone number, the car swerves like crazy, and then we're flying down the road. And before I can scream *I'm tired, I want it to stop*, before anything, we're all looking out the back window as grandfather's easygoing tone of voice disappears, and we're watching to see if we're being followed, listening for sirens and knowing we're only two hours away from the border.

GOBLIN FRUIT

1

'*ve stolen my brother's name. I've lost my own name and replaced it with a dead boy's. I no longer call myself D., but am now M. Around town, some people recognize me for the imposter I am. Others—casting agents, cameramen, other former-child actors who've worked with my brother—become unnerved upon seeing me, mistaking me for the original M., or perhaps not wanting to remember how my brother died. To most people, though, I'm invisible.

As a child I dreamt of fame, imagining the day I'd have to disguise myself in dark glasses to venture out in public. It was tough, that life I dreamt, but it was the price I would have to pay for stardom. But as an adult now in my twenties, I see how far-fetched and dumb and impossible those ideas were, how delusional, yet I'm still enormously saddened at the thought of those young dreams falling out of the sky, crashing to the ground in flames and breaking to pieces.

This sadness at times hides my horror at my actions—my theft of M.'s name, the way I've made it my own. But the notoriety of his name, his tragedy's legacy, seems sometimes like the best thing I have going for me. Life's a bitch in this town, and you do what you have to in order to succeed. Like now, here on the set of this pilot for a cheesy *Star Trek* rip-off—*Z-Star II* is the working title. I'm scared to death this next stunt will fail, but I'm bound by my contract to go through with it, and I can't afford a reputation as someone who doesn't play by the rules. Remember crazy Sean What's-Her-Name—or rather, remember why you can't remember her and why she hasn't worked for years. I don't want to risk my life, but it's not like I have a development deal at Universal. This role, in which I play Chief Petty Officer Ryan Suzuki onboard the Astrolog IV vessel, is the only part I'll probably get this year. And part of me's feeling lucky, grateful that at least in the 23rd century, in mankind's space age future, there are a few decent adult roles for an Asian American actor. Elsewhere in Hollywood I'm a ghost.

As children my brother M. and I, I'm told, competed with one another for attention. During family dinners and holidays, my mother says, we'd both tell jokes and sing songs in Chinese for the amusement of relatives, trying to outdo each other, to win the most applause and laughter. I can't even speak Chinese anymore, but it seems sometimes like I'm still doing my childhood act, only now I'm no longer in the familiarity of the living room with my brother, but alone in front of strangers.

2

The scene takes place on the planet GeminiComm, where a surveillance team composed of Officer Suzuki, Admiral Jon Proudstar, and Lieutenant Rork, an alien of the Nurylian race, have landed to scout for signs of life. Suddenly, an enemy vehicle shaped like a futuristic helicopter hovers above the three of us, giving orders to drop our laser weapons and surrender.

I can't hear a thing above the roar of the whirling blades, not the director barking orders to hit our marks, or the lines tossed off by the other actors. Our dialogue will have to be dubbed in afterwards, if we survive. Gregg, the special effects and stunt coordinator, assured us beforehand that it's all perfectly safe—said he's worked with the helicopter pilot half a dozen times before without incident. But if it's so safe, why are my knees shaking, why can't I swallow?

In my fear my mind abandons me. I'm imagining what the *National Enquirer* will print if this helicopter crashes and kills us. I'm worrying whether I'm famous enough for the news to warrant the front cover. And then I realize the coincidence with my brother would by itself be spooky enough for it to be headline news, or at least a full five minute segment on *Entertainment Tonight*.

It sounds like the perfect storyline for that movie, the one my brother died filming: *the brother of a dead boy, now assuming his name, finds himself face-to-face with the same situation in which his brother died.*

3

My life has been full of strange connections—my brother's past taking life, crossing over into my present.

Here on the set of *Z-Star II* I don't know whether to be comforted or disturbed by the presence of Jack R., a cameraman who also worked on the film M. died on. Jack has admitted his own feelings of unease when filming me, how he can't help but see the face of my brother through the lens.

Then there's J., the young actress. We tested the same day for the new Kevin Williamson pilot, pretending to play parts almost a decade younger than we really are. Neither of us got the role that time, but it's highly possible we'll be cast in some project together someday. We're both survivors. Of the crash, I mean. She's V.'s daughter, the actor who was holding M. when the blades of the helicopter killed them.

4

I'm no stranger to dying. In my day job at the USC Medical Center I develop electromicroscopic photos of human cells from patients who have little hope of surviving. In the photos one sometimes sees hidden patterns—images floating among the ribosomes, nuclei, lysosomes. At the pathology unit we keep a whole wall of these prints, a Rorschach gallery of cellular structures fiercely and beautifully raging out of control. Unexpected, accidental portraits emerge from the arrangement of cell matter in these medical prints: a shape like Kermit the Frog in one photo, and in another a cross, perfectly encircled.

One print in this collection, viewed properly, stares back. The cell matter forms a face with eyes, a nose, a mouth—one of life's little practical jokes, perhaps. The patient, now long deceased, had inoperable lung cancer. I keep a copy of this smiley face mounted in the darkroom of the lab, where I print these $8\frac{1}{2}$" x 11" photos. Cellular headshots of the dead and soon to be dead. I'll usually run a test strip of each print first, in order to achieve the best contrast of the mitochondria, the chromosomes, and the rest of the cell. After putting the prints through the developer machine, the photographic paper—a pure shiny white—emerges a minute later with a pattern of blacks and whites and grays holding the key to the fate of lives. I think the AIDS and cancer patients would be surprised by the beauty of their illnesses, shocked to discover we keep a gallery of their cells' most attractive and exquisite mutations, our exhibit of faces and crosses and half moons on the wall.

It can be gruesome at times, but the night schedule of the job leaves me free for auditions, and all the doctors have complimented me on the quality of my prints. After some time, I've learned to read some of them on my own—I can now detect the most common patterns of ARC cases, or brain tumors. Given the dismal state of my career, the doctors have encouraged me to give up acting, to apply to medical school. I can just see my-self in an aspirin commercial: *I'm a doctor in real life, but I can't play one on T.V.*

I work all night, and in the morning back at my apartment I might eat breakfast with my roommate Angel. If we're lucky, we'll have auditions in the after-noon. With his dark, Latin looks, Angel gets to read for a variety of roles these days: sometimes he's a Cuban drug dealer brought in with gunshot wounds on *ER*, or a Puerto Rican murderer in prison on *Oz*, or a gang-banging cholo on *Law & Order*. Me, the only work I read for requires an accent: Japanese businessmen I'm too young to pull off, or Korean grocers or Chinese restaurant delivery boys (my agent is still bitter that I didn't try hard enough for that Ping role on *Seinfeld*, even now, years after the series has ended).

More and more, I'm feeling my dreams of winning an Oscar slipping away, and I'm no longer rewriting in my head the acceptance speech I've been practicing for years. My self-imposed deadlines for making it have been extended for so long that even I realize it'll proba-bly never happen the way I've always imagined it, com-plete with a Billy Crystal monologue and a tacky Debbie Allen-choreographed production number. I'm realizing my career is going nowhere, and it's about as funny to me as a drive-by shooting, or the signs they have above the coffee machines down the hall at the hospital morgue: one that says REGULAR, and the other DECAPITATED.

5

At night sometimes the noise of low-flying helicopters scares me awake. Sometimes I'm grateful for the intrusion, because I've been dreaming of M.

My dreams about him take many forms. In one version, I'm on the set of his movie and I have to witness the accident—in reality I wasn't there, and didn't learn about it until hours after it was over. In another dream, it's me who gets cast in M.'s part—I die, and M. is the survivor. In yet another version of the dream, I'm the other child actor in the movie—they cast both M. and me in the roles of the children—and both M. and I are killed.

6

Some time ago I came to the realization that my adult roles wouldn't be as abundant as the parts in my youth, when I could always be assured each year of playing Pat Morita's grandson in some project. And then there were the three seasons I was on a syndicated children's program—it took place in a train station overseen by a lecherous adult actor. It's the only part I can remember both M. and I going up for that I won.

Sometimes I look back on my childhood career and I think, hey, it wasn't all wine and roses, but there's no reason for a Mariah-like breakdown just yet. At least I'm not dead, at least I wasn't on *Dif'frent Strokes*. At least I *have* a future.

7

By now, the details of my brother's death are famous. On the movie set for a segment of the film T_____ ____ headed by the director J., a stunt helicopter lost control and crashed. In the scene in question, which took place on a Hollywood studio lot re-creation of Vietnam, the actor V. plays a vet on a mission to rescue two Vietnamese children, one of them played by my brother. Running across the set holding both children as the script directed, V. lost his grip and dropped one of them. That child, X., was crushed to death by the falling helicopter. V. managed to hang onto my brother, holding M. in his arms as the blades of the fallen copter decapitated them both.

Our mother was the one who had to identify the body. At the funeral there was a closed casket. I remember moving through those days lost in numbness— nothing else could faze me.

Our parents' grief was overwhelming, but even so there were plans to be made, days to get through, the restaurant they owned still needing to be run. My mother's face, the face I always remembered being too tired from work and life, grew more weary. Private grief made her face tighten, turn older. There was the public sorrow, too, the hysteria expected of a Chinese mother losing her son that needed to be displayed for friends and relatives at the service. After all this, at home in private, she and my father fell asleep in bed without speaking, exhausted. I didn't even have to argue about going out—seeing them dozing wearily I knew no one would care when I got back. I rode the buses all night, feeling a need to be heading somewhere.

I wound up at the UCLA campus and walked around Westwood, then took the bus to Hollywood Boulevard. The UCLA campus seemed empty, and I realized it must have been a vacation period between semesters. The few students waiting at the bus stop were all Asian, getting in extra study time to keep messing up the grade curves, I suspected. There was also one strange, bearded Asian man talking to himself, dirty and unkempt, speaking riddles.

That afternoon the funeral procession had passed through Chinatown, past the smelly fish shops and dim sum parlors and the newsstands selling newspapers with the calligraphy of Chinese characters. The black limousine my parents and I rode followed a car on the back of which a large, blown-up photo of M. was mounted. It was one of his headshots from the Bessie Woo Agency, the Asian American talent agency that represented both of us. The old Chinese on the sidewalks stared at M.'s photo and whispered to one another in Cantonese and Mandarin, saddened to see a child taken away so young. It was almost Chinese New Year's, close to the Day of Thieves.

Behind us, I heard the sound of trumpets and trombones, the noise of the Chinese Bugle Corps marching in procession. I remember worrying about who was footing the bill for the limo, the musicians, the funeral, knowing that the studio was paying for all of it to persuade us not to sue them.

Now I realize that despite the show and pomp, the Chinese spectacle, all of it was probably very cheap. It was the way of the Chinese here in America. In the living and in the dying, there was the inevitable sweat, the inescapable poverty, the penny counting. The rusted trombones and frayed marching costumes passed down and reused, never new; the rice wine poured in shot cups for ghosts at the graveyard eventually poured back into the bottle; the coins passed to mourners wrapped in bright red paper unveiling not quarters or dimes, but pennies.

I stayed out that night walking and riding buses until morning. On Hollywood Boulevard, walking past the cops and prostitutes and drunks, nobody noticed me or cared. Nobody bothered me, nobody could see me, and I was disappearing inside myself until I was almost, like M., no longer of this world.

8

Leaving the Bessie Woo Agency a few years after the accident was a big risk—I was afraid I would never work again. Leaving had nothing to do with M.; I just felt I could do better for myself being represented by a more mainstream agency, that I would get more parts. I was able to sign with a small well-known agency (not ICM or William Morris but the best I could do at the time) after landing the role of the young Asian sidekick in an Indiana Jones movie—not the *real* one with Harrison Ford, but a low-budget rip-off starring Lorenzo Lamas. I was then the only young Asian actor with the agency, but they never sent me out for the Leonardo roles, or the parts that ended up going to those being groomed as the next hot thing of the moment. My career was stalling, so I thought I'd pull a Jodie Foster—I took out some loans and went to Yale, and I began studying *A Course in Miracles*, began thinking positively and learning to love myself. Four years later and after returning to Los Angeles, I realized that instead of attending Yale I should have gone to a sacred monastery of monks in Burma and studied kickboxing; I should have been practicing my moves for the next martial arts B-movie so that then, at least, I could get some work. I should have been selling my soul, practicing how to look young and successful while being hollow inside.

9

Lately, with my roommate Angel, I've been writing screenplays. I'm even trying to write some Asian American themed films, without much joy or luck. As a lark, I even applied to UCLA Film School and got accepted, but there's no way I can afford it.

So far, Angel and I have finished two ideas. Development Girls of America, please take note.

There's one called *The Mysterious Stranger*—we stole the title from Mark Twain's final book. It's like *The Hand That Rocks the Cradle* meets *The Exorcist*, with an enigmatic, club-footed stranger named John Natas who takes a room in the house of a really good-looking, divorced attorney—think a younger Sharon Stone—with three young children. Soon, all sorts of weird, evil stuff starts happening in the house, until the woman finally realizes what Mr. Natas's name spelled backwards is. Yeah, it's sorta dumb, but with some cool special effects, as a movie of the week it'd be like *Masterpiece Theater* for the WB Network.

The other screenplay we've completed has the working title *Goblin Men*—we're pitching it as the dark side of the *E.T.* story—like *Honey, I Shrunk the Kids* meets *Aliens* meets the Persephone myth as written by Clive Barker. The film starts with the children of a small town befriending some cute-looking goblin creatures hiding in the woods. The children are taught by the goblin men not to tell their parents about their existence, or their hidden village. Whenever the children go out adventuring with the goblin men, the creatures feed them a strange, fruit-like food. (Candy companies should note the possible merchandising tie-ins here.) Pretty soon, after digesting sufficient amounts of this goblin fruit, the children begin to lose their memory and forget their true identities.

The second half of the film is about how the adults fight to regain possession of their kids, who have all now forgotten who they are and are living in the goblin village. The women learn to fire rifles, and the men practice shooting crossbows. The townspeople mount an all-out attack against the goblin men, and finally, after all the goblin creatures are destroyed, their village in the woods burned down, the children return home to the adults.

But here's the neat surprise ending: the children never truly return back to their old selves, and the last scene of the movie ends with the lead actress staring at her son, who's sitting on his bed with a dazed expression on his face. *Honey, what's wrong?* she asks. The camera pans to the child on the bed, slowly focusing on the child's face, a close-up, revealing glazed eyes, still dreaming, his true self lost, stolen away.

10

When I was five and M. was two, I remember there was a crazy woman who lived next door to the laundromat on the corner of the block where we lived. Whenever we were out with our mother and we saw this woman, she was always wearing the same clothes: a yellow windbreaker, a blue blouse, and white pants that flared out at the bottom like bell-bottoms. No matter how hot or how cold it was outside, this woman always had on the same things, as if she had no other clothes.

This crazy woman wore her hair in a ponytail, and she was one of the few white people living in our neighborhood. She lived with an older woman I assumed was her mother, and their small run-down house had Christmas lights strewn around the frame of the front door. These lights were left out all year round, and even in the spring or summer when we walked home at night from the bus stop, my mother and brother and I, passing by the house we saw the colored lights blinking on and off, on and off.

The mother let her daughter roam the neighborhood, and the crazy woman took a special liking to us. Whenever she spotted us in the laundromat or walking outside, she'd come over and pinch my cheeks and talk to my mother. My mother didn't understand English well, and even if she could, from what I remember the crazy woman's remarks made little sense. But the woman had a special fondness for my brother, and she always managed to convince my mother to let her hold him for a few moments.

My mother seemed to trust the woman, handing M. over to her without fear. I was afraid my mother was a little crazy herself, not as protective of M. as she should have been. I was afraid this madwoman would steal M. away from us, run off with him so that we would never see him again.

11

For years and years, for as long as I can remember, there have been screenwriters or producers interested in doing a movie about it. *It.* Our tragedy. The beginning of our sorrows. My brother's fifteen minutes of fame.

We've held out, resisted the lure of the option money. I always thought that if a film ever got made, it would focus on the actor V. who died, or on the director J. who was blamed for the accident. But shortly after the crash, we received contracts from lawyers representing production companies interested in doing the story from the point of view of the children—my brother M. and X., the two Asian child actors.

At the time of the accident, M. was just eight and X. was nine. They hadn't lived long enough to have life stories to dissect and dismantle, for a screenwriter to blow up, exaggerate, distort. The heart of this story is bad luck, bad fate. The pulse of this narrative is tragedy.

Now the story is stale, the years since the crash relegating the accident to the category of old news. It's no longer a sexy topic. Nevertheless, there's always been someone out there able to see the possibility of some money in this story. Last year a screenwriter was developing a script for the sitcom actor T.'s production company as a potential ABC Movie of the Week. My parents and I, we didn't cooperate, but I admit I was tempted—the money for the rights could have paid for film school. With the right connections, I could make my own movies, be the master of the story. Or, at the very least, I could have more artistic control over the way I go about selling out.

But life is strange. Years ago now, when that helicopter went out of control, when our lives were blown apart, studio people seeking to exploit the tragedy offered me the part of my brother in their proposed movies as an incentive for my family to sign over the rights.

I've often wondered what it would have felt like to

play my brother on the screen, what thoughts would run through my head as I stood on a set somewhere in some movie lot recreating his life, his death.

I've thought about how I could possibly get past that moment, waiting as the stunt helicopter flew overhead, wondered whether my fear alone could carry me through that scene without having to resort to acting workshop tricks to display my terror.

And I still wonder about it, even now, years later, when I am much too old to play the part.

12

Here on the set of *Z-Star II* the waiting is killing me. This helicopter scene is like a ghost town for me, a place where M.'s life crosses over into mine. I can't possibly ask for a stand-in to do this scene—this is, after all, a shoestring production, not a James Cameron or Michael Bay movie. All the actors have consented to do their own stunts—consented or else risk being voted off the island, but on paper we've agreed.

I'm shaking. I'm feeling strangely out of step with time, as if I'm outside my own body. It reminds me of a student film I did at Yale, a postmodern satire of cheap foreign movies. We badly overdubbed my dialogue on purpose, so that in the finished movie my lips were never moving in sync with my words. That's how I feel now, scared out of my own self.

I can't help thinking of M. and the accident. Marianne Williamson says that we author our own fear, and

that the fearful self is never who we should be: an imposter. It's a funny thing to think of now, when I'm
using M.'s name, and I'm pretending to be a space sol-
dier in the 23rd century.

*Fear manufactures a kind of parallel universe where the unreal
seems more real than the real.* As the helicopter approaches,
my fingernails are digging into my palms and I'm hoping I'll be alive tomorrow. I'm praying that the movie of
my life won't end without me.

I want this all to be a fiction, something I made up,
something entirely of my own invention.

I want to wake up and have the past eighteen years
be just a dream.

13

I feel guilty to admit now that, as a child, I was ex-
tremely jealous of M. When the agent from Bessie Woo
saw us in the supermarket and insisted on representing
us, it was M. she really wanted—it was our mother who
insisted on me being part of the package. And then, of
course, the bitch at Bessie Woo always sent M. out for
parts before ever considering me.

Once, in revenge, I remember translating the
teacher's comments at the bottom of one of M.'s report
cards to my mother. I remember making up things that
weren't really there: how M. was selfish and didn't
share things with the other students, how he always
spoke out of turn.

After he died, we tried to go on with our lives as

usual. But the Chinese restaurant we owned soon failed, and my parents divorced. No one knew who to blame— the director for his negligence, or the studio execs for shutting their eyes all those years to the dangers on their sets. There was also the agent who let M. take such a potentially dangerous role, the movie crew involved, the pilot, even our mother for letting us go into acting in the first place.

It was all a mystery—there weren't any easy answers. It was like one of those old *noir* films, like *Out of the Past* or *Double Indemnity*, where everything remains all fucked up at the end. I wanted the stupid T.V. ending, the one where the detective finds all the clues and the bad guys get caught and justice is served, and in the end all you have to say is *Book 'em, Dano.*

The failure of the restaurant was also a mystery, but personally I suspected M. had a lot to do with it. My mother displayed his mourning portrait—the one we followed on the funeral day—prominently on a wall. Beneath it there was always incense burning, fresh fruit, a plate of food—offerings for the dead—all this in the middle of the main dining room of the restaurant.

She enshrined him.

It was an act of respect, I understand, but I'm sure the customers felt uneasy. It must have been hard, after all, to enjoy their meal under the watchful eyes of a saint.

14

I wish I could say I felt a sharp, paralyzing pain in my neck the moment M. left us. I wish I could claim he visited me that night, that his ghost haunted me, but I can't. To do so would be to distort the story and change it's significance solely for the little comfort these lies would give me.

15

The one movie that M. and I acted in together, a surrealist art house film about the lives of Chang and Eng, was never completed or released by its British producers. I heard they couldn't find two adult actors willing and able to stay in that costume together for the duration of the filming. When M. and I shot the scenes of the movie depicting the famous Siamese twins as children, staying together in that costume all day was almost unbearable, and I can only wonder how the two Siamese brothers got along during their lives.

And I can only wonder how the remaining brother felt when, in the end, his twin died and he still lived, alone for the first time.

16

Like many people living in Los Angeles, I often find myself overwhelmed by an immense anger, a rage so enormous it brings me to thoughts of violence. In my twenties I'm already suffering from high blood pressure—half the time I'm in a hyper, ambition-fueled frenzy, ready to tear someone's head off, ready to pursue my career with an intensity that would make Courtney Love look shy and unambitious in comparison, and the other half of the time I'm majorly depressed and unable to get out of bed without enormous effort. I just know that if I'd grown up outside of L.A., in the Midwest or somewhere calmer, I'd be more steady and not the poster child for Xanax. Still, I think I prefer this native Los Angeleno frame-of-mind to that of the actors I see at auditions who are so obviously not from here—so calm and relaxed and unaccustomed to struggle—the ones who treat the business like it's some dance recital where everyone will eventually get their turn.

During my rages I'm angry at everything and at everyone—at myself, my parents, the lack of roles for me in the industry. I'm mad at my agent, the studios, my landlord, Michael Ovitz, and all the young actors who get the parts I can never play. Always, though, I find all my pent-up rage eventually directing itself towards J., the director whose carelessness, whose disregard for anything but a large gross and a high return and his enduring reputation as a director of crass middlebrow studio crap contributed directly to the tragedy.

I've never been able to see the movie, of course. I don't think I can, just as I can't fly on a plane without a paralyzing, white-knuckle fear, just as my immense anger at J. will never be overcome.

Marianne Williamson writes: *Forgiveness is like the martial arts of consciousness.* She means, I think, that we can
never successfully revenge ourselves upon our enemies,
that we need to sidestep the whole notion of hating dick-
heads like J., just like a countering move in the martial
arts. It's a nice metaphor, but—for me—sort of ironic.
The only roles I ever *get*, it seems, are *all* in martial arts
flicks, minor one-line parts in schlock like that series
with Eric Roberts as an American kickboxer.

How can I begin to forgive when the whole nature of
my acting possibilities revolves around violence and revenge? Why is my life like the plot engine of an old
Bruce Lee film? I met his son Brandon once, briefly, before his accidental death on a North Carolina set. It was
eerie when I heard about it on *Entertainment Tonight*, the
whole business of a three-generation Lee family curse
as Mary Hart reported. It made me think about the legends surrounding Bruce Lee I believed in as a kid, how
in the future he was supposed to return from the dead.

And it made me wonder also what my brother's
legacy would be in this business, with that horrible history. My brother's death and X.'s and V.'s were supposed to have prevented accidents like the one that
killed Brandon Lee, increasing safety standards in films.
That ought to have been their legacies.

And the bad roles and bad haircuts and stifled ca-
reers of the Asian American actors of the 70s and 80s
and before, I sometimes feel all that history ought to
have created a better place for actors like me. Our passages should have been paid, for a world without the

Charlie Chans, the Suzy Wongs, the kowtowing maids and butlers and delivery boys. What happened, I want to know? How did that older generation let it all slip through their fingers?

I guess everybody was too busy kung fu fighting.

17

When I left for college I wanted freedom from the Chinese I knew in Los Angeles. I wanted to be in a place free of yellow faces, of M.'s ghost, of the sound of helicopters at night.

Moving off-campus one year, I lived in an apartment under some foreign graduate students. After falling asleep at night, I would hear them sometimes through the ceiling conversing in their native language. Hearing them always frightened me, shocking me awake with a sense of displacement that left me feeling like Dorothy in *The Wizard of Oz*, as if I had never gone away to Yale at all but had just been stuck dreaming in Los Angeles. There was a strange, familiar language coming from that ceiling, and it was the sound of Chinese voices.

18

I never saw him in death. That is, I never saw M. dead—there was the closed casket, after all.

So it's entirely possible for me not to think of him as gone. He was just eight years old—it wasn't nearly enough time. Sometimes I feel like I'm keeping him alive, that M. lives on in me. By using his name, I keep him substantial—not dead, not a ghost.

Sometimes I believe I'd do anything to bring him back. Sometimes I wish it'd be as easy as in *Field of Dreams*, that if I wished hard enough he'd return: *If you build it, he will come.*

But I know real life isn't like the movies, and the only thing I can do is say good-bye, I miss you. Rest in peace.

19

I did make it through the filming of *Z-Star II*—the scene was shot without any fiery crashes, without any explosions. All in all, it was what passes for an ordinary week in Hollywood: a week without incident, a week that doesn't contain any material for a future *The E! True Hollywood Story* on your life. Gregg the stunt coordinator took us out for drinks afterwards to thank us for our cooperation. I thought the worst was over, but in the script we received for taping next month, if the pilot gets picked up, the crew of the Astrolog IV do battle with the Warpsmiths of Zambor, a race of genetic firedrakes who, during a fight scene, set Officer Ryan Suzuki on fire. It reminds me of what I heard a studio exec say to Barbara Walters on *Nightline* the night of the last Academy Awards. He said: *They don't call it show* show, *they call it show* business.

20

When I went away for college, the one thing that took the most getting used to that first week of school was the dead silence of the night. I had to learn to fall asleep without the sounds of traffic nearby, the neighbors shouting at one another, helicopters passing overhead. To this day the sound of helicopters still startles me. The noise of their blades shatters my dreaming, erases the images that connect in my mind like the patterns emerging in the lab photos I develop at work that suggest something greater in images of strange faces, encircled crosses, open circles. At night I can dream complete screenplays, whole chapters of novels—all gone from my memory the second I awake.

One night, shocked awake by a helicopter passing too close, I stumbled to the bathroom to piss, careful not to wake Angel in the next room. Still drowsy, I wasn't prepared for the reflection I saw in the mirror: the face of my brother staring back.

He's been trespassing in my dreams. He's taken residence in my thoughts. Maybe he's mad that I've stolen his name. The old-timers—the Chinese who first came to America—hid their true names, adopted false ones; I read this in college in an ethnic autobiography. They did this to elude their enemies and American officials, all those who were potential threats to them.

Maybe M. doesn't know that I mean him no harm, that all of my success is his own, all of it achieved in his shadow. He reduces me to a phantom of himself—his legacy, his memory. I'm left here in the world without him, alone and reminded each night of him as the helicopters fly overhead.

They approach from the distance, like attacking birds. A low roar announces them. The noise of their blades drives needles into my brain, cuts me open to my most vulnerable parts, leaving my mouth dry and my armpits damp from fear. In my bed I can feel them hovering in the sky, hear them as they descend lower, closer, as if they're about to fly through my bedroom window. Their floodlights shine through to the dark corners of the room, revealing nothing: no ghosts.

And then they're gone.

FALLING

I awoke this morning from a dream of falling, entering back into the world just moments before I would've hit the ground. I don't remember where I was falling from, or why, only the sensation of plunging through the air and not knowing where I'd land.

I couldn't picture the ground in that dream; it was a place of ghosts beyond the edge of recognition. Solid and fear-invoking while at the same time hazy and unclear, it was a mystery: the area where one ghost town ends and another begins.

This time it was the dream of falling, and not the dream of the endless stairs, though both are similar. The stairway of the endless stairs has no railing, and on the steps immediately above me two figures are dragging a dead man. The people ahead of me constantly change identities. Sometimes they are people I know well, sometimes famous celebrities, other times strangers. I don't know what is worse, the idea of falling into the unknown off the side of the stairs where the railing is missing, or the thought of climbing the never-ending stairs forever behind the dead man.

Every time these dreams leave me profoundly unsettled—spooked and disturbed—and bring back more ghosts. This morning I thought of Jon—of how much I missed him. I remembered that time when the days seemed endless, the city overwhelming, those days now as distant and out of reach as the memory of a dream in the morning shower.

That sign stands out in my mind, signaling me back. It was the sign of a pie in the sky, a huge neon beacon on the intersection of Vermont and Franklin that drew tourists, hungry locals, and wandering flies attracted to its wonderful light.

The Palace of Pies Coffeehouse listed over twenty varieties of pies on its menu, all baked fresh from their brick oven. It was, for us, a place to pass the time, where we'd spend hours in the old-fashioned booths beneath the light of the huge pie rotating outside the glass windows. Jon's new thing then was bending spoons, and he stole them from the Palace of Pies and anywhere else he could find them. Over the course of an hour every spoon in our booth wound up twisted out of shape. Jon then stole them, hiding them in his large bookbag, and by the end of the year he had accumulated over a hundred spoons. He'd bring them to school, lay them out on his desk, and claim he bent them using mental telepathy like psychics did.

The teachers, of course, always asked him to put his bent spoons away, never failing to suggest he apply the powers of his mind to more useful things like his homework. But Jon was never practical, someone prone to hopeless fixations on the irreverent, the inconsequential. He'd become obsessed with Michael Stipe's mumblings on an REM song, spending days trying to decipher the lyrics. He'd get eyestrain staring at the ghostly figure captured standing on the balcony on the cover photo of the *Hotel California* album, wondering how it got there. On maps of Los Angeles he would attempt to locate the ghost areas—the fake streets and blocks drawn on maps for purposes of distinguishing copyright. Then he'd try to drive into one of these non-existent places, as if he could lose himself within those phantom spaces created by the cartographers.

Once, after almost swallowing a fly in his slice of French apple pie, he decided to rename the pie restaurant Palace of Flies. He pursued this scheme relentlessly, meticulously redoing a copy of the restaurant's advertisement with the new name, then getting the school newspaper to run the ad in its April Fools' issue.

That restaurant was full of insects, it's true—the huge, spinning neon pie outside drew them with its glow. Sitting at our booth we'd see hundreds of them hovering around the sign, some flying too close occasionally and getting zapped. They moved without purpose, attracted only to the brightest light.

At a quarter to midnight the head waitress, both her makeup and nylons running, would stumble to the cir-

cuit box and with her long, painted nails flip off the
switch controlling the sign. The pie in the sky's spinning
would slow and its glow dim, then it'd stop turning altogether and its light would fade completely. The flies
remained hovering in the air, confused by the sudden
change. Then, in an act of faith and with great purpose, they'd quickly reorient themselves and fly, blindly
and crazily, towards the nearest light.

That year, the year we both were taking classes at
UCLA, was one of Tuesday and Thursday drives with
Jon. The classes got us away from our high school in
Silver Lake, giving us permission to leave at lunch and
get to Westwood via Sunset Boulevard, past Tower
Records and the restaurants on the Sunset Strip. The
path we took wasn't any quicker than the freeway, but
Jon enjoyed driving his car on the fast, twisting turns of
Sunset and the even more difficult curves on Mulhol-
land Drive in Beverly Hills.

He also liked showing off his car. It was a used red
Porsche his father gave him and he spent his weekends
working on it. He loved the car and took excruciatingly
good care of it, scowling when I forgot and slammed
the door too hard or brought ice cream back to the car
from Baskin-Robbins. It was small, a two-seater, and
sitting inside it one felt the motions of the engine working and the wheels moving as we raced to and from
Westwood.

In autumn when the sun disappeared before six,

we'd look up and see the sky glowing bright, odd colors
and feel the air become that distinct combination of
cold mixed with the strange warmth of the Santa Ana
winds blowing in from the mountains. Because it was
his car, Jon more often than not won the repeated argument over whether to leave the car's top on or off.
When we drove back home with the wind blowing in
our faces, the sun would set every time almost precisely
as we turned onto Mulholland Drive. Jon would turn
on the headlights, his favorite part of the car because
they rose up and did a little flip, just like the racecar on
the *Speed Racer* cartoon.

Mulholland was famous for being a road where
many a driver had lost his life. Jon always tempted
fate—one of his tricks was to close his eyes while driving, trusting the soft impact of the wheel in contact with
one of the shimmering divider disks to indicate to him
when he was too far outside his lane. This unnerved
me, as did his other trick where he would steer with
only his knees.

Without my glasses I could barely see the objects on
the side of the road illuminated by the headlights, casting shadows in our path. The houses and buildings
around us on Mulholland were imposing in their
grandeur. They rose up like fortresses.

A television producer, famous for his one-hour teen
dramas, was attempting to build the largest mansion in
Beverly Hills. The house had been under construction
for years, and from the road we saw the framework
going up slowly each passing week. We also saw the

Beverly Hills Hotel, an elaborate building nicknamed the Pink Palace that had served throughout the years as the site of many sordid Hollywood tales. It was here where the eerie photo with the phantom guest on the balcony was shot for the *Hotel California* album.

Towards the end of Mulholland stood a gated house, enormous and grand, distinguished by the stoneboys found in its elaborately cultivated garden. Every time we passed this house I glanced at them, life-size statues of black stone carved to resemble groundsmen working in front of the house. They were grouped together in pairs: two stoneboys bent down at the base of a large tree, another pair working in a patch of flowers, a couple raking leaves together, and the two closest to the road, who stood with their backs turned and their heads tilted towards one another as if in conversation.

As we sped along Mulholland Drive I envisioned in the dark that the shimmering disks of light in the middle of the four lanes were signaling us out of the Hills so that we might not be captured and frozen there for life like the black stoneboys. We kept our eyes on the road ahead, not looking back for fear of being caught and turned to stone.

The stoneboys never moved, frozen in the same position when night approached as when we sped by them arriving in the daylight. Someday, I imagined, they would break free of their enchantment and awaken from their dreaming. In the last rays of the day's end, their black silhouettes began disappearing into the coming darkness. I dreamt that in a few hours, under the cover of the night, they would escape from the garden into which they had blundered and been imprisoned, that they would be able to carry out the escape they practiced over and over in their heads, the one they planned in secret with their twins in whisperings inaudible to those who only spot them while passing on the road.

🦋🦋🦋

It's a Saturday afternoon and Jon has driven us to the Ralphs Super-Super Market on Santa Monica Boulevard—the huge one that stocks caviar and Godiva chocolates, where it's not uncommon to spot T.V. celebrities. But stargazing's not what we came for; the water balloons are in the toy aisle, next to a huge cage full of large plastic balls, and the funnels are in the kitchen utensils section. As I get these, Jon sits in the car waiting.

A skinny blond boy about my age stands in front of me at the checkout line with a bottle of hair conditioner, waiting for the checkout girl to finish with the woman in front of him. She's buying three large bags of Alpo dog food. I look at the headlines of the tabloids at the counter. I read that Martians have landed in the Soviet Union, that a Kansas girl has given birth to a dog, that Elvis Presley still haunts the halls of Graceland.

And a little later we're at a party at a house up in the Hollywood Hills. The insides of my ears vibrate. In the corner some guy has his head right next to one of the stereo speakers as he nurses his drink. I recognize him from television: he played the kid sidekick on a fantasy show that used to air on Sundays. It was canceled some time ago, and then years later his co-star accidentally killed himself on the set of a detective series with a prop gun.

Some people here are drinking, others are getting high, and some are doing nothing. Jon and I have just come over from another party, the one we needed the water balloons for. A girl in Los Feliz we knew from our English class had invited us to a Christian party—there was Ping-Pong, and people tried to start a water balloon fight, but no one really wanted to get wet. In the end everyone sat in a circle in the living room and some guy studying to be a minister spoke. He told us how it didn't matter if we weren't the best student or the most popular or wealthy, that what mattered most was sustaining one's faith and being satisfied with what you had been given. He asked everyone to think privately of the things they were most thankful for and led a prayer. I couldn't think of anything and in the middle I looked up and of course caught Jon's eyes, and of course we both had to stop ourselves from laughing out loud.

So typical, and looking now across the room at him even though I'm staring straight at him I'm not sure he sees me this time. In his mouth he has a length of plastic tubing attached to one of the funnels we brought. Someone is burning some stuff through the wide end of the funnel and Jon is inhaling the hit through his mouth. A fat girl next to him is screaming *Go! Go! Go!*

I leave the room and head out to the backyard, where I can still feel the loud dance music coming from inside. The smell of the liquor and drugs have followed me through the sliding glass doors. I look down at the pool and I'm surprised to find it empty, its bottom stained green from algae and littered with brand-name trash. From this vantage point in the hills I can see the city below and the sky above it on this strange day, where it's raining in some places and sunny in others. In one part of the city a man is washing his brand-new car, sudsy water running into lush green lawn as the sun shines above. In another corner an old woman looks out from a window of her peeling apartment at the children playing out among dead grass and broken bottles, calling them in as the rain begins to fall.

Looking upwards we see the body framed against the sky, poised in the air for the briefest glimmer of a second before beginning its great downward fall, followed by the splash of body meeting water.

These diving facilities were constructed at UCLA for the 1984 Olympics, the year everyone in L.A. had eagle T-shirts and pins bearing the five ring emblem. On campus waiting for our classes to begin, Jon wants to play video games at the student center. I remember an essay he wrote in eighth grade, an exercise in personification. *Don't put your dirty cigarettes out on me because I don't like baths—they're bad for my software*, he wrote. *Don't push too hard on my buttons or I'll get mad.* Jon was the new kid in school then, and his earring and hair and Melrose thrift shop clothes didn't leave people with the impression that he was such a computer geek.

At the university Jon was enrolled in a computer science course that involved higher mathematics. He was writing programs with endless equations, programs that would never stop, running into the future forever unless overridden by a secret master command.

Jon was serious about this work, but his mind wandered when it came to what would happen in his own future. We would both be graduating soon, and he had no plans. By this time, I had already accepted a scholarship to Columbia University so I could get away from my family and from the city. Jon wasn't too happy either with his life in L.A., but he thought he could go on living the way he did forever, that nothing would ever change. He was still believing he'd never grow old.

I remember now, now that I haven't heard his voice or seen him in so long, that that time when he was wrestling with the laws of endless equations was when he was most . . . not *happy*, but *content*. There was a certainty and perfection in that realm of math and science that could not spill over into our own lives. It was that ageless perfection we admired in the arc of the diver, the steady rule of gravity that brought body into water one hundred percent of the time.

Jon applied this same sense of sureness to the computer program he finally perfected, a program I didn't really understand but that I can sort of describe. Any number, no matter how small or how large, could be entered at the start of the program, and the computer would begin calculating a string of equations based on that number, over and over and over. I think the equations were processed outside of binary technology, calculated simultaneously instead of serially—or something like that. Sums and remainders and quotients spilled out into eternity, the digits filling endless rolls of printing paper cascading onto the floor and the equations running forever, never ending, no, never ending.

I spent the week before I left for college with Jon. We saw movies at the Beverly Center; ate at a restaurant housed in a big, converted train; ate at another one shaped like a giant hamburger; drove up to the observatory in Griffith Park.

So many times before he had driven me where I needed to be, and there were those times when he would be so tense that I knew something was bothering him, but I wouldn't know whether it was me he was upset about or something else. I never said anything, although I knew I should have. Sometimes you let those moments pass, secure in your faith that the opportunity will come again.

We spent the night before I flew to New York driving around, and at one point Jon said he wanted to take me somewhere. There was a man he wanted to show me, he said, a man who stayed outside Thriftys drugstore, which was open twenty-four hours. They sold ice cream there, too, and Jon said, —Let's go get some ice cream. I'll buy.

It was two in the morning and there were only a few hours left before Jon would need to drive me to the airport, but when you are a passenger it's hard to say no sometimes. On the drive over I learned the man Jon wanted to show me was an old transient without any arms or legs. He stayed in a dirty wheelchair in the parking lot of the Thriftys, where occasionally people gave him money for food. Jon said that the man appeared not to have a face as well, and that he was the scariest thing he had ever seen.

We drove to Thriftys and searched through the parking lot, looking for this man with no arms, no legs, no face. Jon cursed: —Shit, he's not here tonight, and finally gave up after circling three times. There was a lot he seemed to want to say, but not enough time. I sat there looking out at the empty parking lot, which was lit by the streetlights and the full moon. Orion and the Big Dipper were in the sky. —Do you still want to get ice cream? he asked. And seeing him there knowing I might not see him ever again was like seeing someone you know in a different light for the first time.

Later, as we sat in the parked car with our ice cream cones, I spotted, hidden in the corner by the dumpsters, the old man we were searching for. I didn't see his face—I was scared of what I would or wouldn't see there. Under the lamplights his body appeared like a sack of dirty laundry, a collapsed tent held up by shoulders bent over, bent over to shelter the heart from any more pain.

• • •

I kept the ticket stubs, receipts, and other items from that last week in Los Angeles as reminders of that time. I kept these things in an empty cassette box that once held my tape of *Astral Weeks*—Jon had borrowed it and lost it. He and I lost touch after I left. Years later, in New York, I opened the cassette box and fingered the items in it after receiving a call from someone who had heard a rumor that Jon had died—from drugs, or in an accident, or from a combination of the two.

It was one of those things I knew certainly could've been true, but I didn't really want to know for sure. I didn't want to face up to the truth. Jon, I remembered, never had a firm grasp on cause and effect, believing life to be like one of his endless equations that would never stop. But when confronted by it, Jon had a serious respect for death, like with the dead boy, whose face had haunted our dreams for endless nights years ago.

This is how I first heard of the dead boy:

My eleventh grade counselor had his secretary call me into his office one day, looking quite serious and sad when I stepped in. —I understand you knew the boy well, he said. —What a horrible thing to happen.

Responding to my look of complete confusion, Mr. Sherman elaborated on the story of the *unfortunate boy who took his life* the day before, and we both soon concluded we had a case of mistaken identity.

Leaving his office I heard Mr. Sherman yelling at his secretary, and by the time I could tell Jon at lunch what had happened, news of the dead boy had spread across the campus. Kenji Miller, though he had not known the dead boy, was incensed. He considered suicide a sin, thought anyone willing to take his own life must be insane.

Later, the exact circumstances surrounding the suicide began to surface.

The dead boy's mother found him first, on the floor of his bedroom, the gun resting close by. Initially the family wanted, desperately, to believe that it had been an accident, but the evidence proved otherwise. It was speculated the dead boy was ashamed about not getting into the college of his choice, or upset by his family's harsh reaction to his above-average but not perfect grades. Another story focused on his intense loneliness, another on rumors of a secret love. The dead boy, it came to be known, was a quiet but well-liked member of the Rifle Club and a photographer for the yearbook and newspaper.

In its next issue the paper ran an obituary, and Jon was the reporter who volunteered to write it, never mentioning the cause of death in his article. We never spoke about it.

When yearbooks arrived at the end of the year an extra page with a photo of the dead boy was loosely tucked into each volume, the photo having been sent too late to the printers to be properly bound. By the end of the day, the floors of the campus were carpeted with endless images of the dead boy's face, his faint smile trampled over by the feet of people moving on to lives he would never share. Some took the photos and contemptuously ripped them to pieces or poked pencils through the dead boy's eyes. Both Jon and I kept ours in their place at the back of the book, and in the years to come I would be uncomfortably reminded each time I opened the book of the dead boy's face and what his eyes hid.

I could say that Jon's respect for the suicide was a healthy regard for the memory of the dead, or kindness to the surviving family, or simply proper protocol.

But what it was, I think, was a sort of envy, a longing for that promise of certainty. In the dead boy's act there was no measure of the unknown, no uncertain ground in dreams or endless stairs leading nowhere.

Knowing Jon, the rumors of his death could very well have been of his own making.

In the same yearbook with the photo of the dead boy there's a whole series of pictures with Jon listed under his alternate persona, his pseudonym—Jonathan Hemlocke. I never really understood the point of the joke, or why he took that particular name, but he went through elaborate measures pursuing it, popping up in photos for clubs and committees he didn't belong to.

He was the same way when examining each page of the yearbook, searching feverishly for a photo capturing the face of the undercover narc who had posed as a student for a few months of the fall semester. The whole thing was over—the narc had set up some students and busted them outside the campus one weekend, and it was all announced over the P.A. sys-

tem during homeroom on Monday morning. The dealers were caught, the cop's cover blown, and Jon was
simply lucky he wasn't part of the crowd targeted. The
cop then disappeared, and we were left to wonder
whether we had ever seen him, talked to him, crossed
his path.

But Jon wouldn't let him vanish so easily. He was obsessed, pursuing his detectiving with a rabid intensity,
like a young Matlock on crack, hunting for that one
image of the cop, some evidence of his existence, his
face in the background of a photo, as if capturing that
would somehow mean something.

I don't know what it was he was looking for.

🦎🦎🦎

Around Christmas the malls in Los Angeles are always
packed, drawing people in with bright promises. The
December chill has set in, that bite in the air all that
indicates winter in Los Angeles. I am back for a while,
but I have no urge to find Jon, just as I have no desire
to stay. This time of the year especially, people tend to
lose themselves to a belief in transformations, the hope
of possibilities.

Individual acts of faith sustain them, and sometimes
they are broadcast out to the collective city. Every year,
within a few days of Christmas, you can be sure that
a miracle will transpire; on the evening news Tricia
Toyota or Laura Diaz will announce that a struggling
L.A. family has received a sign from above. The news

cameras will flock to the scene, the archdiocese called in to confirm it officially, and soon the family will, with the aid of protective neighbors, bar the news media from filming for fear that whoever has granted the miracle might take it away if it is shared.

I haven't once seen actual footage of any of these minor miracles, only the newscaster telling me to accept her word that she witnessed it, or reports that the whole neighborhood saw it. These revelations take many forms—a shadow in the shape of a cross appearing for days across a sidewalk, an image of the crucifixion seen through a dirty bathroom mirror, the face of Jesus Christ formed in a burnt tortilla.

None of these miracles have ever been captured on video, as if faith refuses to enter the modern age.

Then in January I'm heading back to New York and I'm giving directions to the shuttle van driver on how to get to the airport. On the busy intersection of Virgil and Jefferson stands a new Korean Methodist church, where a white neon cross competes with the glow of the city's street lamps and traffic lights. We are passing by the church in the far right lane. The white glow from the lit cross draws in the night insects, a buzzing halo of wings. The neon cross speaks to me with its electric hum, but I cannot decipher its code. As the light ahead changes from red to green, I can't decide whether to turn right or move straight ahead.

.   .   .

On the *Astral Weeks* album there's a song with the lyrics *And I will never grow so old again.* . . . Hearing the combination of Van Morrison's voice and the words—that sense of loss—gets to me every time. And although that song was recorded before I was born, I think that sentiment is as close as anything to what I think I'm trying to approach with this story.

When Jon drove me to the airport the morning I last saw him, the streets were empty and dark. I had a five-thirty flight and we had stayed up all night looking for the faceless man at Thriftys, then just talking and driving around. Heading to the airport the streets looked unfamiliar and dangerous in the dark. Few other cars appeared on the roads, and it felt spooky—as if the highways were haunted.

Jon had problems seeing the road ahead, and the Speed Racer headlights didn't help much. Passing under bridges and overpasses we held our breath. There had been earthquakes the week before, and we were afraid of aftershocks, or another bigger quake, which would have meant the earlier ones were foreshocks. It was always confusing to keep these things straight—to understand them, yet not to fall all to pieces from fear.

When the plane took off I noticed it first moved away from land, towards the ocean, before circling back east. It flew away in order to return. In the air looking down, everything looked almost exactly like a tiny map. I wished Jon were sitting next to me, able to see everything with some distance—to see in the air just how small the city was, how everything seemed so insignificant, like it couldn't possibly touch you.

Later, going through the items I saved in the cassette box from that last week—the movie ticket stubs, the receipt for the ice cream cones, the cheap ring we found in the grass at Griffith Park—my hands shook when I touched the check stub from our lunch at the restaurant shaped like a train. You see, there were many different versions of the rumors of Jon's death—in one he was high and crashed his Porsche, and in another his car was hit by an oncoming train when he tried to drive around the crossing rail at the train tracks. The version that made the most sense to me was a combination of the two.

Holding the check stub from the train restaurant I tried to stop myself from shaking. I told myself, *You don't know anything for sure.*

The restaurant was a converted train selling hot dogs and burgers, with luggage racks above the tables. The windows next to the tables slid open. The check stub I'd saved said: WE'RE GLAD YOU'RE HERE.

I put it away. I had no time to try to make sense of all this. Maybe it was better not to know for sure, to wake up before I hit solid ground. It was better not to know where Jon was, better to think he had vanished into memory, fallen off the face of the planet into one of those phantom areas in the hidden heart of his own private map. In the years ahead he would be a ghost in the corner of my eye, the face I think I recognize for a split second in the airport before disappearing at the gate of the flight leaving for Bogotá, or Tokyo, or Peru, the face I cannot turn back to look at for fear of being caught, frozen, between the dead and the living.

EMPTY HOUSES

It's a mystery to me now how it happened, but for a long period of time I lost the ability to have memories. During those years without memory, I wasn't particularly concerned with much besides getting through the present. I knew how pioneers must have felt, those who looked to the west for their futures— men and women who settled Los Angeles, battling the heat, the arroyos, the natives, to construct a city of myths and dreams; immigrants past and future betting on a plane ride, a boat trip, a run across the border.

Don't look back.

In *A Course in Miracles* there's an exercise that teaches you that the past is over: the lesson is it cannot possibly affect you anymore. An auxiliary lesson is that one's capacity for greatness relies on the ability to forget the past and the future. It is a formula for living wholly in the present.

On the other hand, there's my friend A., who's always thinking about anything but now. *Remember when . . .* , he'll begin, unless he's making plans for his own death.

He says: *When I die, I want my body to be buried beneath a fruit tree, deep down where the roots will grow through my bones, and every spring when the tree harvests and the fruit grows ripe, all the people who knew me will take a bite and say, —Yeah, he's tasting real good this year.*

And I know A.'s idea isn't original, that he took it from some seventies movie, but I believe his sentiments are heartfelt and worth repeating nonetheless.

🐾🐾🐾

I remember as a kid reading Superboy comics where Superboy had all these super-powered friends in the distant future who called themselves the Legion of Super-Heroes. All of them were teenage heroes with special powers who banded together to fight crime and wear neat costumes. Superboy flew into the future with his super-speed whenever he needed to see these friends, and in the future, of course, he could read the history books and newspapers and surf the internet and find out what would happen to him eventually, and even when and how he would finally die.

Of course, all his friends discouraged him from learning too much about his future, knowing how that would really fuck up his mind when he had to return to his present. At times, they'd travel back in time—back to Superboy's era—to help him whenever they knew Superboy would be facing a villain or a danger that he alone couldn't handle. Sometimes Superboy was able to go back in time with them, go back in time to his own history, and it was always so incredible and so amazing to me how Superboy could go back in the past to save himself.

Whenever the Legion of Super-Heroes entered the 20th century to help Superboy with a kryptonite menace or a magical villain, they rode back into the past on the timestream in a time machine shaped like a giant bubble. Once the mission was completed, though, before they said their farewells to Superboy and went back to their own present, the teenage heroes were always kind enough to use a futuristic device to erase parts of Superboy's memory.

They did this so that he wouldn't have the burden of living and knowing his own death and his future. The Legion of Super-Heroes knew that it was impossible to have to remember some things, even for a Superboy.

🐾 🐾 🐾

Driving on the freeway the other day, I spotted a message alongside the road that surprised me so much I was sure I was hallucinating; that it was on an electronic billboard for a Don Kott auto dealership made it even more odd to see the words MEMORY IS MORE INDELIBLE THAN INK flashing on the side of a freeway. This was just days after a magnitude 6.6 earthquake, and in my head I added: *more indelible than bricks and freeway columns and apartments and houses, too.* That sign haunted my mind all day, so much so that all I could think of was to check on my way back whether I'd only imagined it. But the sign was still there, and it haunts me still now, even as I sit down to write this.

🙚 🙚 🙚

I've been wondering about those magical stories we all remember hearing as kids, the ones about lost children in the woods and giant pumpkins and peaches, the ones where evil men get turned to stone or to ashes and everybody winds up living happily ever after. Are those stories any less real because in real life there are no prince charmings and no magic wishes granted, or is it simply real life that's broken and needs fixing?

Maybe it's true that once upon a time a boy left his house at the edge of a dark wood and got lost, and ended up voyaging out into the world upon an odyssey of discovery. And maybe that boy journeyed for years and years, and along the way he encountered a witch who melted into water, and another witch fallen victim to her own poisoned apples dying on the red leave-strewn floor of the woods, and a king who was really his father who turned to stone in the end, and a fish that could talk, spinning wild tales about lost magic books and the good fortune that finding them would bring. And maybe other times on his journey the boy encoun-tered a forest full of animals frozen as glass shining in the daylight, and a girl's red cloak smeared with animal feces and blood abandoned beside a haunted lake, and separated twins with a psychic connection, and goblin men who tried to seduce him with their goblin fruit. And maybe after all those adventures, the boy was still not sure what would be the big surprise at the end of his quest, what magic key he might find that would unlock the answers to all the puzzles in the vast wilderness of his heart. And maybe that boy was me, and maybe one day I wandered upon a town, finally, a strangely familiar one reminding me of the one I left many years ago. And as I pass through this town I encounter, block after block, row and row of empty houses —lights are on in each of them, but no one is home. And so I walk around this ghost town, and in the area where the town ends and the woods begin I spot a single house with the sprinklers turned on in the front garden. And when I approach this house and walk to its door, before I can even knock it opens up and before me stands my twin, an older version of myself. And before I can open my mouth to speak he comes over and embraces me, and he says, *I've missed you, it's been so long.* And then he holds me in his embrace for some moments, and I can hear and feel his—my—heart beating, and then he says into my ear, in a voice I recognize, *Welcome home.*

BRILLIANT
DISGUISE

My father calls me in the night. Stumbling out of bed, sheets wrapped around me, I manage to grab the phone in the middle of my answering machine message. I've been dreaming for hours already, but my father doesn't know this. He really doesn't know me at all.

—Your mother wants you to come eat dinner, he tells me. I do this every three months or so and that's all I ever see of them, even though I live only twenty minutes away. I hear my mother in the background reminding my father of the time and date he should tell me. I figure she has him call me so that the two of us get to talk more.

After writing the date down in my appointment book, I head back to sleep, but the call has already ruined any possibility of a peaceful night. Later in my dreams, I'm being pile-driven and double-teamed and figure-four leg-locked. A sleeper hold is applied to my

neck. I wake up pounding my hand against the bed—
one, two, three! Later in the shower, the irony is not lost on
me: I *woke up* after the sleeper hold.

The rest of the day I feel a vague sort of resentment
toward my father for giving me those dreams, and for
not knowing he shouldn't call so late. What he should
have known is that I go to bed early because at six each
morning I rollerblade along the bike paths in Griffith
Park.

I skate to the office, too, and I'm glad that I don't
have to use my car because of my driving phobia,
which, like the bad dreams, I have my father to thank
for. He did such a bad job teaching me to drive—not
telling me what to be careful of until *after* I made the
mistake—that I've been traumatized for life. But the office isn't too far from my house in the Silver Lake Hills,
and part ownership of the business means flexible
hours.

When I get in I find Imee, our receptionist and secretary, down on her knees next to the fax machine, furi-
ously smashing bugs with an old telephone book.
Lately, the bugs have been everywhere in the office.
They're only ladybugs, which to me aren't so repulsive
as cockroaches or locusts, or those potato bugs that
occasionally show up in the parking lot. Our accounting office is located in a residential neighborhood,
about four blocks from my old high school, and except
for the tax season we rarely see any walk-in customers
so it was strange when homeless people started wandering in, trying to sell us eggs full of bugs.

Some philanthropist had started a program where destitute people could pick up the ladybugs for free— they came packed about a hundred each inside silver egg-shaped containers, which were then sold for a dollar a piece. The eggs were sold to home owners, who needed the bugs for their gardens after years of malathion spraying had virtually depleted the natural ladybug population that guards against aphids and other garden pests.

When it rained, these homeless bug vendors wandered the streets wearing shiny, metallic-looking smocks they had been handed by the government, guarding their precious eggs from the wetness beneath this makeshift silver rainwear. Their shiny outfits dragged along the ground so that they seemed to float as they drifted slowly down the wet streets, looking like ghosts from some distant, unnamed future: an era of silver clothes and silver eggs and constant rain.

None of us in the office ever bought any of the eggs, but I can remember clearly the one man—boisterous, smelling of liquor—who dropped one in our reception area, releasing hundreds of ladybugs inside the office. The bugs flew out from the shattered egg like a red mist. They flew out and entered the air like a cloud of toxic memory, and in that moment my mind flew back to the year I'll always remember as the first year of the sprayings, my last year of high school, and the year my father lost a cage match.

·   ·   ·

I remember waking up one morning that year, opening a window, and smelling that something was not right. The night before, insect spraying had begun in a part of the city close to where we lived, the section of Echo Park inhabited mostly by Latino and Asian immigrants and other members of the working class. We lived in a section of Los Angeles that had no name, but it was somewhere between ethnic Echo Park and upscale Silver Lake, a prime real estate area where my parents dreamed of living someday. They saw other Asians living over there in their perfect three-storied houses, new cars parked outside, the kids off playing tennis or at cello lessons; they wanted that for themselves. I guess I did, too.

That year an infestation of fruit flies was threatening the agriculture of the whole state, so proposals to spray even urban areas like Los Angeles were mandated. L.A. residents balked at the idea, of course, rallying to keep their homes outside the spraying territory. During the initial spraying everyone seemed to think it might be possible to get away with spraying just those areas people didn't seem to care about, even though the people in Echo Park weren't the ones with the imported fruit trees growing in their backyards.

I became involved in the lobbying effort against the spraying only because of my school friends, the ones I envied and never invited home to see where I lived. The chemical being used was malathion, a powerful insecticide that people feared would lead to unexplained health problems like the soldiers exposed to Agent Orange.

I heard the helicopters coming in the distance when I went to sleep the night before. I wasn't sure then whether they were the copters carrying the spray, ones haunting my dreams, or just regular ones like those that passed overhead each night shining thick beams of light across the streets below.

In the morning I was sure they were real, that they had indeed released the chemical. Days later I would hear stories on the news about homeless people becoming ill after direct exposure to the malathion. Even that morning I clearly saw its effects in our area with the stray dogs, once threatening, now staggering lost and confused down the street, and I felt it in the air that it hurt to breathe in.

When my father went out in the morning to start up his car, he smelled it too. He was a large, quiet man who rarely shared anything with me, my mother, or my two younger brothers. I knew he smelled the poison because of what I heard: curses in a mix of English and Chinese, the slam of his car door, the start of the engine, and the sound of him driving off to work.

My father didn't have a traditional job in the Asian American sense—he wasn't an accountant, or an anesthesiologist, or a restaurant owner. He wasn't a scientist, or a judge, or a brain surgeon. He was, in fact, a wrestler, although this too, like other parts of his life, was rarely discussed. I had grown up not really knowing or caring what he did for a living until I got into middle school, when I began to realize how different he was from other fathers, the lawyers and doctors from Los Feliz and Silver Lake whose kids I now took classes with.

Then I started watching the television matches on Saturday afternoons, when I was alone in the house and no one knew what I was watching. My father wouldn't have approved of me seeing him at work; he never, ever talked about his matches—what he did, or how he prepared. I found out what little I knew from the television screen.

If his wrestling career was supposed to be a secret, it wasn't a very well-kept one. He never brought back to the house any of the wrestling stuff I saw on the television screen: not the nunchaku weapon he used illegally to beat Sergeant Power, or the kendo stick he employed to hit Mamoo the Magnificent and win the Intercontinental Title, or any of the costumes he wore in the ring. I looked all over the house, but I couldn't find any trace of the white oriental powder he sneakily threw in the face of Rowdy Roddy Piper, or the exotic, blinding green mist he blew out like a dragon from his mouth to blind Hector Santana and pin him. I never found him out this way, but seeing him in action was easy.

Most of the matches took place on a Friday night. The fans were wild: shouting, spitting, giving their favorite villains the finger, and jumping frantically up and down at the prospect of blood spilling in the ring. These were the same people, I thought, who invented Monster Truck racing, who believed shit was pronounced as a two-syllable word.

After being taped, these matches were broadcast on television Saturday afternoons on a UHF station. We had an old set, and to get the UHF channels you had to spin a knob below the normal 2–13 channel switcher. The knob was faded yellow plastic, with the numbers printed in an arc. The wrestling program was found somewhere between channels 50 and 55, you could never tell for sure, and at one-thirty every Saturday they showed wrestling straight from the Olympic Auditorium.

My father could be seen almost every week in some match during the two-hour program, which was interrupted at intervals by cheaply-filmed commercials for used cars, loan sharks, greatest hits albums, and vocational colleges. Right there on the screen I could see him doing what he never talked about at home.

He wasn't very good at keeping secrets, because I also knew that he spent the weekend gambling at the race track, at Santa Anita or Del Mar, which is why—with my mother and younger brothers gone visiting her sister in Monterey Park on Saturdays—I was alone in the house and able to watch whatever I pleased. This gambling, I guess, was where all the wrestling wages went, why we were never able to move to Silver Lake like we wanted. This was before pro-wrestling hit the big time, back when it was confined to places like the Olympic Auditorium on Pico Boulevard in a forgotten section of Los Angeles. In the wake of the Cyndi Lauper heydays, after the numerous Wrestlemanias, the action figures, the video games, and the rise of The Rock and Stone Cold and other recent megastars, wrestling headlines at the big sports arenas and tours nationally, but back then, it was possible to make just enough to lose it all at the track, which is what I assumed happened each week to my father. He never talked about the losses, but I could tell. He hid his racing forms in a bookcase that no one used, in the shelf that held the unread volumes of the *Food, Cooking & Nutrition* encyclopedias we got from Aunty Mei-Mei. He thought no one knew he hid the forms in-between the *T* volume—tiramisu, tortellini, tortes, tuna—and the combined *UVW* volume—uneeda biscuits, vichyssoise, watercress, wontons.

Money had always been a worry, I knew, and when you grow up with immigrant parents, pennies and nickels and dimes add up to small fortunes. In his rare talkative moments, my father told stories of how it was before I was born, of how my mother had worked in a meat factory until one day one of her co-workers accidentally sliced off their thumb on a machine. I always wondered what they did with that thumb, but I never asked. I still cringe thinking of the story: how the lady had to be taken away by ambulance, and how my mother decided then to quit. So I'm not surprised my mother didn't say anything about the gambling, because at least he managed to keep us where we were, at least she didn't have to work as much anymore.

I don't know much about the beginning of my father's wrestling career, I only know what I've seen on T.V., and there isn't much to tell. It's all basically the same story, told over and over again with slight variations. In the black and white world of the wrestling stage, with its pantheon of heroes and villains, my father always played the heavy. He was the inscrutable one, the devious Oriental who will do anything to win and who can never win fairly. Usually he's pitted against some all-American type, the kind of dude the fans wave the flag for. He plays the threatening jap, the one who's booed, who's told to go back to where he came from. If he wins, he does so by using some trick he learned in the Orient—a deadly karate chop, or mysterious fumes or white powder, or an oriental variation of the nearly fatal sleeper hold.

For a number of months that year my father, the wrestler, was embroiled in an ongoing conflict with Fabulous Frank Fortune, the latest longhaired blonde hero of the ring. It went like all the other rivalries did— the ones with Dashing Dave Dalloway, Macho Man Arnie Muellens, Ted "Venice Beach" Miller, All-American Brent Powers, Kris Von Erick, and others too numerous to remember. A series of matches escalated the conflict, some won by Frank Fortune—always fairly— and some won by my father. The matches my father won were always done so illegally, of course. He threw powder in the eyes, or pulled the trunks for leverage, or employed an illegal object in the ring. The animosity between the two wrestlers would inevitably explode into an all-out blood battle—the usual conclusion to such situations in that world—culminating in a much-hyped fight to end all fights topping the wrestling card for the next week.

The stories with all the previous blue-eyed wrestlers ended neatly enough with the defeat of my father, ending the foreign reign of terror in the pages of that chapter of the book of professional wrestling. But the rivalry between Fabulous Frank Fortune and my father—who went under the name Mr. Moto in the ring, even though we're Chinese—escalated far beyond that. It got so out of hand that instead of the usual title bout to end the feud, the conflict led into a loser-leaves-town match.

The day of the match was much anticipated. I saw it the day after it happened—on tape, on T.V. I watched the fans get riled up behind their boy, Fabulous Frank. There he was in red, white, and blue tights.

The outcome was as expected. Going through the match blow by blow is useless, because it was the same old stuff—full of teases for narrative tension, with someone the audience could identify with and a sound defeat to trumpet the theme—never, ever a cliché in wrestling—that good always wins out over evil.

After the match I was scared. I worried about my mother and my brothers. I didn't know what we would do without my father's wrestling income, and I sure didn't want to lose a thumb in no meat factory, either. For weeks I was waiting for my father to break the news to us: that either we were losing our shitty house, or that we would have to move to white-trash Tennessee so he could join the wrestling circuit there.

One Saturday, however, after weeks without Mr. Moto appearing on the wrestling show, a wrestler calling himself the Yellow Angel made his debut. He wore a yellow mask with just the tiniest of holes for the eyes and nose and mouth, so no one could tell who he was. The mask was embroidered with a small red cross on the forehead, and around the rim of the Angel's left eye was a blazing red flame design, like a fire burning out of control. The Yellow Angel fought both bad guys and lesser-known, less-liked good guys, beating both types. His fame grew quickly.

I wasn't sure whether it was my father underneath that mask or not, and to this day I cannot tell you one hundred percent for sure one way or the other. I do know that if it was Mr. Moto underneath that mask, he appeared a lot happier being an anonymous wrestler than the despised yellow villain. Assuming it was my father, at least now he was permitted to use the moves he wasn't allowed to use previously, could show everyone that he could wrestle scientifically, just as well as any of those guys. Putting on that mask in some way freed him, moved him beyond the kung fu shtick he was forced to play before.

You could probably predict what happened next. It was destined, maybe, or at least scripted. In the Yellow Angel's ascent up the ladder of the Wrestling Federation he was intercepted by none other than Fabulous Frank Fortune.

Meeting up with a clear-cut good guy, and a popular one at that, the simple justice of the wrestling universe mandated that the Yellow Angel become a villain. At least he wasn't race defined, so when the Angel cheated to win a match he didn't breathe green fire into his opponent's face or hit him with a kabuku stick. The Angel was able to use the old-fashioned American methods of throwing a chair, gouging his opponent's eyes with an illegal metal object, or simply hitting him upside the head with the bell clapper.

Every Saturday I sat glued to the set, watching as the drama unfolded and the conflict between the Angel and Frank Fortune intensified. The commercials between matches offered a break to run to the refrigerator or the bathroom, but usually I just sat and watched. An announcer promised the amazing success of Ginzu knives, used in the Far East for centuries, or a call button for when you've fallen and can't get up.

Many of the commercials advertised used car dealerships, and the most prominent one featured a man with a cowboy hat named Cal Worthington who appeared with his dog Spot. Cal promised to stand on his head if necessary to sell a customer a car, and each commercial ended with him doing just that, as the camera moved from the upside down Cal outwards to project the wider picture of the whole car lot.

Cars of every shape, size, and model filled the screen, glistening underneath a hot California sun, until the picture stopped expanding and it appeared like the whole world was filled with empty, used cars just waiting to be bought.

The helicopters came in the middle of the night before the big match, the day of the Angel's unmasking. The conflict between the Yellow Angel and Frank Fortune escalated as you might have expected, marked by a series of illegal wins by the Angel in which he was aided by other villains like the Russian, Ivan Kruschev, and the African American wrestler Big Bad Teddy Brown. Fortune and the fans got fed up with the cheating, and finally it was proposed that a match be fought in a steel cage to prevent any possibility of outside interference.

One on one, Fortune vowed, he would destroy the Angel, he would rip the mask from his face.

I was in my bed, dreading the outcome of the Angel's next battle, praying for his good fortune. In the distance I heard the sound of the blades spinning, the roar of motors as the helicopters approached. Then I saw the light shining through the window, which I had made sure to shut for the night. I waited for them to arrive.

The vibrations rocked the house. The windows shook, and through one window—illuminated by the helicopter's searchlights—I could faintly see the spray of chemicals descending.

It took almost a minute, and then it was gone. It didn't end there. For hours afterwards I heard the helicopter in the distance, spraying and re-spraying other areas.

I fell into a deep sleep that night. In my dreams grotesque animals transformed by their exposure to the malathion roamed the streets with terrible objects clenched in their jaws.

In the morning none of this had come true. The city officials were mostly right, and the sprayings continued, though in the future they were confined to specific areas, and the helicopters were no longer employed.

We had lost, it seemed, despite all the lobbying efforts, and it felt like a terrible defeat. It felt like being thrown over the top rope, sprawled on the concrete floor and unable to get back in the ring while the referee finishes his ten count.

The next year I went off to college, and there I was more concerned with graduating and making some money than with any political causes. Caught up in passing my courses and working my way through school, I watched silently as around me other students played at being radicals—the militant minorities who called themselves oppressed people of color while their parents paid their tuition and MasterCard bills, and the out gays and lesbians, the recycling geeks, the socialists, all free to be activists on an elite campus comfortably shielded from the real world. It seemed like a play, where the actors fell into their roles and got lost within them, and at times I wanted to join in but I had more immediate concerns.

My father the wrestler couldn't care less what I was doing, and he gave me little support as I struggled through college and then business school. When I returned to Los Angeles with my MBA—a new person, or so I thought—all my time was concentrated at the office, working my way up to part ownership. That last year of high school became a distant thought, a year devoted to a knee-jerk cause I only half believed in, falling in step with the dance of the moment, one which other people forgot as different problems consumed the city.

That year the officials had said that the homeless were at no risk, that malathion had no obvious detrimental effects upon humans. In the morning everyone awoke, the smell in the air reminding them of what they thought they had only dreamt the night before. Pets were let out, and cars were started. Before stepping into their cars, though, most people stopped to remove any coverings they'd placed on them the night before, because the city had cautioned that the chemicals, though reportedly harmless to people, might damage the paint.

Let me describe the wrestling ring on the day of the match. A steel cage was constructed around the ring— an inescapable prison as large as history—that would surround both the Yellow Angel and Fabulous Frank Fortune. The two would wrestle inside this cage, with the referee the only other man inside to ensure no possibility of outside interference. There were handcuffs at each of the four corners of the ring, handcuffs a wrestler could employ on his opponent for a maximum of five minutes before the referee unlocked him. They called this a Texas-style-revenge cage match.

The match started out pretty evenly, until the Angel took the advantage by throwing Frank Fortune through the ropes and into the hard steel bars of the cage.

The Angel followed up by reaching into his trunks

for a foreign metal object, which he jabbed into Fortune's face. He then drove Fortune into the ring post, afterwards raising his arms up in victory to taunt the crowd. The Angel, I saw, was clearly the villain now, and although I didn't want to think it, that spelled only one outcome.

Dazed and confused, Fortune stumbled back to his feet. He came back with a roundhouse punch, stunned the Angel with a head butt, then executed a staggering flying dropkick.

Fortune regained the lead, placing a hammerlock on the Angel before moving his opponent into position for the unbreakable Boston Crab hold. The Angel miraculously broke loose, however, amid the crowd's boos, and performed a flying head scissors on Fortune.

Then, after dazing Frank Fortune with a series of forearm uppercuts, the Angel applied his infamous sleeper hold.

This should have been it. This was the hold the Angel had used in seven previous matches to put to sleep and defeat seven different opponents. This should have been the end—lights out, *one, two, three* . . . but the crowd was behind Fabulous Frank, shouting encouragements to keep him from losing himself to sleep. Frank struggled, but the Angel held on, until suddenly, in a burst of incredible strength, Fabulous Frank Fortune propelled the Angel backwards into the steel cage.

The Angel was dazed, hitting his head against the metal, and Fortune managed to get him into one of the handcuffs. The cameraman got a close-up of the Angel's hand. In my recollection of the scene, sometimes I picture my own hand on the other side of that cuff, and sometimes I see the long silent history of a people. On the screen, though, there was nothing on the other end; it was linked only to the ropes.

The crowd grew louder, screaming for the removal of the Angel's mask. I saw the red cross on the mask, the left eye ablaze. Fabulous Frank teased the crowd, removing the laces slowly, bit by bit, as the back of the Angel's black hair was slowly revealed. I knew then that the mask would come off, that the time had come for the Angel to come face-to-face, in that steel cage, with who he really was. And I knew it was all an act, that it was an elaborate show choreographed like the circus and rehearsed like a soap opera. The blows when the wrestlers hit one another never left any bruises, and assault charges were never filed when a wrestler was battered senseless in the ring and had to be removed on a stretcher.

The crowd cheered on Fabulous Frank Fortune, calling for the mask's removal. I watched as the laces of the Angel's mask were finally undone, as Fortune moved in and began pulling the yellow mask off the Angel's face.

I watched as the mask slowly came off, and then I turned off the set. I didn't need to watch. I already knew the story.

Sometimes we build our own cages, sometimes we set ourselves free.

All of this happened many years ago, so you have to forgive me if things didn't occur exactly as I described them. I was younger then. Frank Fortune, I am sure, was not nearly so much the cliché that I present him here as being. He was a much more complex man, all the wrestlers were, as much blinded and trapped in their roles as my father. But in memory we tend to recast our stories with heroes and villains, with clearcut, black and white symbols of wrong and right that do not exist in our real world.

In the years since, so much has happened.

The Cold War's end has redefined the face of wrestling, bringing forth an age once undreamt of. The Russian villains who once terrorized the square circle—wrestlers like the Russian Nightmare and Ivan the Horrible—have all disappeared, gone in the blink of an eye.

A few resourceful ones—the ones who used to do battle with the likes of Frank Fortune, Hulk Hogan, and All-American Brent Powers in the featured matches—have been reborn, often taking on new names, new identities. Nikolai, the ex-Russian Terror of Leningrad, has renounced his past and joined forces with Brent Powers to capture the prestigious tag team title. Ivan Kruschev, we now learn, was never really from Russia, but from *Lithuania*. He's become a fan favorite, renaming himself Captain Freedom, and he now enters the ring to the music of Springsteen's *Born in the U.S.A.*

With the Russians all reformed, my father has been in high demand. He's even bigger now, swelled up from years outside the ring. He no longer wrestles, but remains in the wrestling world as a top manager. He's the man you see with a big briefcase of money, now playing the Japanese heavy threatening to buy up all the wrestlers. He carries a cellular phone to keep in touch with his investors in Tokyo, and occasionally he'll deviously interfere in a match, tripping up one of his wrestlers' opponents, or knocking them in the head with his briefcase. The stories don't change much, they simply evolve with the times.

The fans of wrestling have evolved also. The wrestling crowd has grown more upscale, more mainstream. Now, when I see the wild fans on t.v. with eyes thirsty for violence, they look like the well-groomed sons of my clients. Frank Fortune's red-blooded fans are called Fortune-Maniacs. They appear for a moment like well-behaved boys out enjoying the theater, until my father or some other despised villain appears, and then they shout their obscenities, saliva flying, their faces twisted monstrously to resemble Halloween masks.

The targets of their hate have evolved, too, a whole new generation of minority wrestlers in line to collide with the likes of Fabulous Frank Fortune. Fortune has continued with his grappling career, and despite his receding hairline he's one of the top stars of the merchandising cottage industry that's arisen around pro-wrestling. You can buy Frank's image on anything from T-shirts and posters to bandannas, acrylic mugs, and toothbrushes; last week, I even saw him appearing on *Celebrity Fear Factor*. In the aftermath of the Hulk Hogan steroids scandal, and the tragic deaths of Andre the

Giant, Kerry Von Erick, Brian Pillman, and Owen Hart, Fortune has proven himself to be a survivor, a member of the old guard of still-active ring veterans still fighting for screen time while the sport evolves.

He'll have to contend with the new generation of wrestlers, youngbloods like Rockin' Ricardo Ramon, the dangerous Cuban immigrant threatening to swallow America whole. —I don't want just a stinking crumb of the American pie, he snarls. —I want the whole thing! First I'll take the Federation title belt, then all of America!!

Then there's also the Cherokee, Hunter Goingsnake, fighting in the squared circle for the dignity and ghosts of his ancestors and for his dreams of a new Native American nation. He enters into the ring like a man possessed, with a determination so strong that every time I see him I'm struck with a sense of déjà vu: that look, the face like my own face years ago, except that I was determined to do everything to avoid the ring and move away from what my father was.

My own dreams have materialized, somewhat.

I've managed to move to the Silver Lake Hills as my parents only dreamed of doing, living on credit and hope, on the edge of things. There is a house, empty except for me. The third floor has a balcony that overlooks the city, and I sit there some nights to read, or just to look out at the sky and the stars, the helicopters and planes passing by. At times I look instinctively toward where our old house was, but I can't even see it. It's too far away.

—Why don't you talk to your father more? my mother asks me. —He is your father. What did he ever do wrong to you? I can't answer her.

I do know that we meet in dreams. When I get those wrestling dreams, I find myself with my father in the ring, and I help him with his cage match. In this one alternate universe version of myself, I've followed in his footsteps and become a professional wrestler. We're a cross-generational wrestling family, like the Von Ericks, the Harts, the Guerreros.

Together in the ring, we can beat all our foes. We are invincible. We have them on the ropes, we have them pinned, but then we change the rules. We call for peace, for an end to all the fighting. (We can forgive, but we won't forget.) We shake hands with our opponents in a gesture of unity. And together, we all walk out of the cage.

WATCHTOWER

This is what I remember: it was the late seventies, a summer when the Santa Anas blew through without warning, the mysterious warm winds leaving raised temperatures and scorched, dry lips in their wake. The heat, the smog, and the air we breathed in and out each day seemed inescapable, as if we were all trapped in this world, where everything bad recycled itself into each passing year.

I was eight then and Greg Montoya was my best friend. We lived across the street from each other, and a block away from Lockwood Avenue Elementary, the school named after our street. My family had recently moved there from our old apartment one block away from the Vista Theater where Sunset and Hollywood Boulevards intersected, where we had lived for years and where I had grown up literally in the shadow of the Church of Scientology which loomed high in all its blue splendor down the street.

That summer I was spending as much time as possible at Greg's house. It was like paradise to me, only slightly imperfect, if at all—paradise as seen through the distorting panes of a glass house. If that image of family life at Greg's house wasn't perfect, it was the best example I saw, free from the fighting, the yelling, and the financial worries across the street at my house. On the radio that year Fleetwood Mac's *Rumours* album dominated the airwaves. *Don't stop thinking about tomorrow*, those lyrics repeated endlessly, but that particular vision of the future never passed clearly through my own head.

I was young and clueless.

The days passed, each one resembling the one before, days us kids hoped to stretch out to prevent the sun from leaving, the night from coming in. Sometimes after dinner, we were allowed back out, into a California night that was never too cold. In light sweaters or long sleeves, we danced out into the street, years before the dealers came in on the corners. The weather was mild, our worries light. Despite any problems at home, we believed that for the time being we were safe.

We had faith.

Greg came from a family of Jehovah's Witnesses. This faith was the source of their identity, and it permeated their home as thoroughly as the air they breathed. Entering their house I couldn't help but breathe in their faith also, have it enter into me like the tainted city air outside.

At first the name of their religion scared me, invoking images of secret organizations like the FBI or the CIA. But in due time I was invited to their Saturday Bible readings, where the family and their guests sat around the kitchen table reading passages aloud. It was like school, I thought, with pencils and yellow markers handed out to underline and highlight the important words and phrases.

It felt good to be a part of them, united by the pure language. With the Bible as our principle textbook, together we were learning to speak the words of Jehovah. I knew I was moving away from my family, crossing a border by learning this language.

I saw the strange words, a language so unlike any I had previously known or heard, as something so new and marvelous as to seem like the only possible truth, a truth that might free me.

At school Greg's faith set him apart. He passed up chocolates shaped like Santas and Easter eggs, missed out on Valentine's Day and Christmas cards. He skipped school on days we held holiday parties, and during the Pledge of Allegiance each morning he remained seated or left the room, never reciting the pledge that included the phrase *one nation under God*. When we had to write about our favorite heroes, he cited the Lone Ranger and Jesus Christ.

To his credit, Greg remained firm, rarely budging from his duties to his faith. He did, however, give in to a

fascination with evolution, speculation directly contra-
dicting creation theory. We shared stories about the
distant age of dinosaurs and huge flying lizards; we
speculated on mythical creatures like Big Foot, the
Abominable Snowman, and the Loch Ness Monster.
These creatures, we decided, were the last survivors of
their time, left lost and wandering as cities and highways sprouted up around them. They inhabited our
dreams and fantasies, took shape in the dark spaces of
our minds.

Our belief in Big Foot and Nessie grew, kept alive in
our club of two. Between the two of us we sustained
our belief, our theories reflected off of each other and
made stronger. Alone, we would have given up speculation, surrendered to common sense, and returned to
the world of the easily explained and proven. But together we assuaged one another's doubts and kept alive
the mysteries—the dream-inspired stories.

We trekked long blocks under the sun to reach the
Pets & Tropical Fish Shop on Sunset, where we rarely
bought anything but stood enraptured for hours watching the fish and other sea creatures. Mythical sea horses,
sea turtles, and small, red polka-dotted frogs captured
our eyes. An array of fish swam in lighted aquariums,
darting quickly away when we tapped the glass walls of
their world. We paid special attention to the aquariums
housing the electric eels and the water snakes, modern
day cousins, we thought, of the Loch Ness Monster.
They swam in glass cages lit by phosphorescent bulbs,
where humming pumps spilled endless bubbles into

a world of water. The store itself smelled of kelp, fish food, and seawater. Muted rays of light bounced off the blue and red pebbles that lined the tanks, spilling into darkened corners and creating the atmosphere of a strange, secret world, one lost from the gaze of the city.

In time, though, we were politely ushered out into the street, the glare of sunlight striking our eyes as we passed out the door. Heading home we passed the bar next door—the Silver Saddle Saloon—another secret world. Dangerous-looking men in boots and worn jeans entered the doors into the darkness, letting out into the street whiffs of the world contained inside.

Once, on the way back home, we came across a bag of tropical fish lying on the sidewalk, the kind with rainbow designs on their sides and long fins like sailboats. The bag with these sailboat fish had apparently popped, and the fish abandoned on the sidewalk where they struggled within the plastic, their sharp fins attempting to poke through. Cooking under the hot sun, they gave a few last desperate flips and flops on the sidewalk as they drowned in the air.

The heat was often unbearable those days—the sun crisped your hair and darkened your skin until it came off in dead rolls in the bathtub when scrubbed hard with soap. Greg and I played games of cops and robbers with water pistols, ending eventually with one of us dumping a bucket of water over the other's head.

Returning to Greg's kitchen, we ran glasses full of ice cubes under the tap. The glasses had cartoon characters on their sides—Tweety Bird, Sylvester, Yosemite Sam, and Wile E. Coyote and his lifetime enemy the Road Runner. The ice made sharp, cracking sounds as water filled the cups.

Out in the back of their house the Montoyas had a large guest room next to their garage. The fully-furnished room contained a sofa, a king-size bed, and an air conditioner. Behind the curtains of one wall, huge sliding glass doors opened out into a large tract of land, empty except for long blades of grass swaying in the wind.

The door to this room was never locked, but we never entered through it. We preferred to pass through a paneless window adjacent to the garage. Climbing on top of crates in a garage filled with oily car parts, garden tools, and dozens of tepid six-packs of RC cola and Aspen soda stacked in cardboard, we were able to squeeze through this window into the guest room. We never took the easy way, always making things difficult to test ourselves.

One of the conditions given to us in using the room was to not jump on the huge bed, so of course we did this every chance we got, reaching hands out to touch the ceiling before we landed on the springy mattress to jump higher, again and again. Exhausted afterwards, we turned on the air conditioner to the highest setting, lying silently on the bed listening to the sounds of the cool air entering, the tense bedsprings creaking underneath our weight.

Along with the *Watchtower*, the official Jehovah's Witness magazine *Anouncing Jehovah's Kingdom*, Greg's mother kept the room stocked with copies of children's magazines, publications with titles like *Dynamite!*, the *Electric Company Magazine*, and *Highlights for Children*. *Highlights* was the best of these because it had puzzles where readers had to find objects hidden within an illustration. For example, a girl's dress would be cleverly drawn into an image of a tree, or a dog would be ingeniously drawn to blend into a sketch of a car. Greg's mother encouraged us to read these, but usually we had other things on our minds.

Occasionally we slid open the glass doors and ventured outside into the tall, unkempt grass that reached our waists. Trampling through this small jungle, we kept watch for snakes and other creatures made solid by our imagination. The field was home to thousands of ladybugs, red dots in a backdrop of green. One day, for reasons unknown, Greg decided to take a tin can and collect them. I found the colony of them living in the grass repellent, so Greg ventured out alone. Promising to return soon, he opened the sliding glass door and headed out on his adventure.

I watched him for a while, as he bent down into the barrier of grass to seek out the ladybugs. As he moved into the center of the green field, I spotted him by the white of his T-shirt. I soon lost track of him as he trekked out to the borders, out near the edge of the next block's sidewalk. He seemed to blend in and disappear into the field, like an object in a *Highlights* puzzle. I sat on the bed, waiting for him to return. The air conditioner hummed, releasing currents of icy air that collided with my exposed skin. I laid back and enjoyed the sensation, eventually falling asleep.

When I awoke, Greg had returned through the glass doors, carrying with him the can full of ladybugs. I snuck a quick peek into the can and saw a blur of wings and spotted backs. They varied in shade, from a dull orange-yellow to the brightest cherry red. They made little noise—they didn't buzz madly like a hive of bees or like angry hornets. Instead, we knew their existence by the sensation of them moving busily about in the can, bouncing off the sides in a frenzy of activity.

I thought of other insects we could have captured. The ladybugs were easy, relatively slow-moving and safe. They weren't like the dragonflies that appeared suddenly on summer days, shooting through the air like winged missiles. It was said that in China kids caught them and tied strings around their tails, flying them like kites. I've never seen that happen. They were carnivorous, and scared me. Even dead ones on the ground appeared dangerous, a thin steely body with large eyes. Alive, they flew noisily through the air like angry war helicopters departing a foreign country, images we'd seen as children on the television screen each night.

Ants we lorded over like gods, watching their every movement. We placed obstacles in their pathways to watch them react, took magnifying glasses and concentrated the sun's rays to burn dry leaves above their homes. With a hose we flooded their tunnels, driving them out carrying white eggs and the winged queen mother, moving their colony across the land, heading west. We made them into pioneers, set them out into the borderlands to rebuild and rename their concept of home.

Butterflies we watched throughout their life stages, from caterpillar to cocoon to winged monarch. We saw them in each of their many lives, building new habits and homes from scratch. Each death was never an ending, but a metamorphosis.

But the ladybugs would never change.

Their fate was in our hands. We could let them go or we could keep them. That was all.

Greg carried them out to the street, pondering our next move. We thought of leaving them in various gardens along the way, where they could build new lives. We thought of releasing them from the top of the highest apartment we could find, so that they could fly towards the sun. We thought of many things, but we were stopped before any of that could happen.

Seiji Okamoto and his little brother Marshall sat outside on the steps to their apartment. Their father owned the building, and they attended a private school instead of going down the street to Lockwood Elementary. Seiji asked us what we had.

—Let me see, let me see, Marshall cried out. He was four. Greg didn't see any harm in it, so he passed the tin to Marshall. Marshall gripped it with his little fingers, opened up the lid a crack, and looked in.

He stared and stared.

—Okay, give it back now, Greg said.

—Marshall, give it back, Seiji echoed.

—No, I want. Marshall sounded adamant.

He wouldn't let go, even as Greg pulled. Then, as Greg made one last attempt to retrieve the tin, that world we had captured and held in our hands, Marshall freed them, opening up the lid and overturning the can.

A dazzling waterfall of reds and oranges and shades in-between showered down onto the sidewalk in slow motion, a slow parade of winged marchers falling through the air. Most just fell onto the sidewalk and remained there to get their bearings, but a few brave ones tried immediately to take flight. They were dazed from hours without light or fresh oxygen, and they weren't helped by the humid air devoid of any lifesaving breeze to help them take off. A few lucky ones did manage to escape, however. These were few, and I hoped that in taking to the air they did not glance back at the many who remained, did not see what happened next. For in that next instance, before anyone could stop him, Marshall approached the red blanket spread out across the ground, picked up his feet, and stomped over all of them.

No, they did not leave a pool of red on the sidewalk.

Instead, it was more like purple stains faded into the ground, like juice on fingers after peeling dark ribor grapes. Afterwards, Greg kept asking, —*Why? Why?*

Marshall cried and seemed repentant, but, as they say, the damage was done. All but a few were dead.

Hours later as the sun was setting, I saw Marshall and Seiji's father come out and connect a green water hose to the outdoor faucet. He wore cut-off jeans and a Raiders T-shirt. —Marshall is inside. He'll be punished later after dinner, he told me.

Mr. Okamoto turned on the faucet, watered his plants and washed his car, and then moved on to the sidewalk. The purple stains came out easily. The water was strong. The bodies washed free from the concrete to mix with dirt and leaves, broken glass and cigarette butts. The water formed a small river, heading east. The remains of our departed red ladies were carried away by the current, with the litter and leaves, all flowing into the gutter.

In the silence of my bedroom some nights, in my secular house, I tried praying. I was young and afraid.

I wasn't sure how to do it—whether you actually spoke aloud, or said the words in your head—so I compromised by whispering simple desires, soft words muffled by the sounds of street traffic passing a block away. A picture in the *Watchtower* led me to begin speaking to God. Greg showed me the magazine when I asked him why he did the things he did.

It all came down to one big day in the future when the world would end, I found out. In the *Watchtower* an artist's depiction showed what it would be like for believers and for the unsaved. Earthquakes, floods, and fires all raged at once—buildings fell, houses burned, and hundreds of people lay injured or dead on the streets. It was obvious from the drawing that all the dead and injured were nonbelievers, those who had not prayed enough or followed the teachings of the Jehovah's Witnesses. The artist depicted a number of the unsaved who had skillfully managed to avoid the disasters around them, now all desperately praying for the first time in their lives. —Jehovah will know they don't really mean it, Greg assured me. The caption under the drawing warned: *But these would not be saved. It was too late to begin.*

Those who had been praying all along were shown content and unharmed, while around them the non-believers burned, died, or futilely prayed. They smiled, the expressions on their faces saying *I told you so*, like lottery winners having endured for years the ridicule and disbelief of friends. I wanted to be among these people, to be one of the saved, so I began praying.

I kept copies of the *Watchtower* under my pillow to help sustain my faith. Having the *Watchtower* there comforted me; the magazine itself, I noted, stated each issue in a section outlining its purpose that the magazine *comforts all peoples with the good news that God's Kingdom will soon destroy those who oppress their fellow men and that it will turn the earth into a paradise.* I wanted to be there, not stuck here in this life, so I prayed.

But eventually, I gave up. I needed some image— some clue—of the one who would bring about this transformation of the planet. —Nobody knows what

he looks like, Greg assured me, then mentioned something about *mysterious ways.*

But what larger-than-life figure could I equate with
the destruction and renewal that was, I was told, to
come in our lifetime?

No image had held my amazement since years earlier when I was a boy who still believed in Santa Claus
and in his parents, who occasionally cried while watching T.V. Waiting with my mother once for the RTD bus
downtown amid the towers, swap meets, and panhan-
dlers, I spotted—perched in the sky—a mighty figure
looming over all the dirty streets and the crumbling
buildings. He was standing on the roof of a restaurant,
watching over everything from his tower—even directing the traffic, it seemed. He appeared all-powerful, a
looming figure with the muscled body of a man and the
head of a chicken. He was a bizarre and incredible
hero for the city—he was the Chicken Boy.

He saw it all, perched so high you had to stretch your
neck up to gaze at him. In the restaurant below him,
people munched unaware on fried wings and legs,
while outside people hurried past the street preachers,
the guitar strumming musicians, and the old women
mumbling to themselves. Above it all, he stood unfazed,
his feet spread, his strong arms bulging from his shirt,
hands resting on his hips.

He haunted my dreams.

Later, I would search for more plausible signs of di-
vinity, thinking that they too were hidden within the
popular culture, bad taste, and humor of everyday,
ordinary lives. They were there before our eyes just

waiting to be spotted, I thought, like the answers to a puzzle in *Highlights* magazine.

One day I was home alone when the telephone rang. A radio program had randomly selected our number for a widely-publicized contest, and to win thousands of dollars I had only to correctly answer one multiple choice question. The announcer asked me if I was excited. I responded like I thought I should, feigning enthusiasm like the prize winners I saw on T.V. game shows. What I really felt was fear, fear of what would happen if I did win, fear that I didn't deserve such good fortune. I hung up before he could even ask me the question.

This is what I can't forget: on the day the world ended, I learned, the true believers would ascend to heaven. I saw *Watchtower* illustrations of how lucky drivers would be sucked up out of their cars into the skies. This sucking up trick expedited matters, it seemed, as the now driverless cars then plowed into other cars, preferably those being driven by nonbelievers condemned to hell.

I wasn't sure about the fairness of all this. I questioned whether a just God would allow such things, whether there wasn't a cleaner, less painful way to get rid of the atheists.

After a few months of trying to learn all I could about the Jehovah's Witnesses, I gave up more confused than ever. Greg and I remained best friends, but I stopped going over to his house for Saturday Bible study. Two years later Greg announced that his family would be relocating, his father taking a new job in Fort Worth.

The summer Greg moved away to Texas was one of the hottest ever recorded in Los Angeles. The hot air made people lazy and forgetful, and fires were a common occurrence. Fire engines raced through the streets daily, their sirens screaming. Sometimes we smelled the smoke before we heard the sirens.

On the day of one of the worst fires, which killed twenty-one people in a single apartment complex, black smoke poured out into the sky, obscuring the horizon. Greg and I were outside, and we climbed the steps of the highest apartment in the neighborhood to get a better look. We saw everything over a radius of five blocks, including the burning apartment building three blocks away. There, it was normal for people to live crowded together, multiple generations of large families of up to nine or ten in unsafe, low-rent one bedrooms.

The black smoke kept floating up into the vast expanses of blue sky. The fire burned for hours, until the sun set that day in a surreal, chemically enhanced pastiche of angry purples, absurd pinks, and mournful peaches. As the light began to fade and the last of the fire was extinguished, little fluffs of dirty white began falling from the sky.

This was what snowflakes must be like, I thought.

—They look like tiny angels, Greg said. As they continued to fall, we saw them more clearly. They were gray ashes, little tiny gray ash angels, falling down over all the buildings and houses, the streets and the cars and the trees, and us boys. They got caught in our hair and clothes, and we reached out to catch them in our hands. I caught some in my right hand, and smeared the grayness between my fingers. The ash angels spread into the crevices forming my prints, where their smell would stay for weeks.

SEVEN SWANS

1

Once upon a time I was one of seven brothers. We were seven chinese brothers, with one sister and horrible in-laws, including our uncle, the evil magician, who hated us. One day this magician, completely unprovoked as far as I know, cast a spell upon us. We were seven brothers transformed into seven swans. To save us, our sister could not speak a word and had to sew seven shirts, shirts that would turn us back from swans to boys. *Save us, sister*, we cried, wishing. We wished for our return, for our blistered feet that fit snuggly in worn old tennis shoes, for the sunburned arms poking out through faded Ocean Pacific T-shirts with the familiar holes, but our sister could not speak. I was a black swan. Years and years passed, our sister sewing in silence, around her feet spirals of thread like snakes. Eventually I moved far away to a big city. Every day now I stand on subway platforms, crowded with

other people like me not born in the city but here looking for a little bit of magic. Before a train comes you
can hear and feel it before you see it—a clattering, wind
rustling in the tunnel, then flickering light approaching.
Along the tracks rats who may have once been princes
scurry for cover. Listen closely, something good is coming, and be prepared to receive it. Something great can
happen, if you believe in it.

2

During my first years in the city I worked in an old office building undergoing construction; a new wing—
the last design project by the Italian surrealist architect
Grimaldi before his freak death in a Milan elevator
shaft—was being added. As we sat in our cubicles we
could hear hammering and sawing but could never tell
from where, the sounds eerie and distant. Once the new
building wing was completed, the building seemed possessed by the late surrealist architect's spirit. Elevators
had a life of their own, taking riders on wild trips up
and down the building, the doors refusing to open; fax
lines in the new wing were crossed with those of the
nearby medical center, and streams of confidential patient information poured through the fax machines all
day long—surgical notes, time of death certificates,
prescriptions written in doctors' scrawling longhand; at
sunset the sunlight streaming through the enormous
window panes that served as the eastern walls of the
new wing created a hypnotic effect that made walls dis-

appear, and the resulting glow was so inviting that everyone who saw the weird light felt like leaping out the windows; finally, the lobby of the new wing was decorated with winning art contest entries from the local public schools, works by child artists that all uncannily shared universally bleak themes and imagery— a closet opening to display a row of hanging corpses, a girl with a gun pointed to her head, portraits of people with cancerous growths, and painting after painting of beheaded bodies and disembodied heads. In the nearly two years I spent in that strange building after the new wing opened, I would sit in my tiny cubicle pretending to work while in the background elevator alarms set off by trapped passengers sounded and people tried to avoid staring at the eastern walls. I felt a profound separation from my coworkers while confined within the walls of the cubicle I entered each day, and I was reminded of how, in the most populated city in the country, a man once concealed himself on purpose within a prison of bricks he built, trapping himself by his own hand like a fairy tale in reverse and living there for the rest of his life. I felt daily the need to retreat, to return to a quieter beachside life in California not crowded with so many people and faces and personalities so hungry with dreams and ambitions held inside for so long until that hunger burns into hard hearts like stained glass. In quiet moments I dreamt of the star-sailor, my hero from picture books, who flew higher and faster than anyone else, beyond Earth even, a visitor of stars, a hitchhiker on meteor storms, a stowaway riding

pirate ships manned by space ghosts, always moving. I
dreamt of a mild-mannered freelance reviewer by day,
who at night transformed himself into his true identity—a sailor of the stars, flying the space winds like
Kirby's Silver Surfer, or floating listlessly from planet to
planet, carried by a kite of seven red ravens. He was always moving toward something good. Like everyone
else in the city, he was an alien, exiled as a child from
the dust of a dead exploded planet, sent by rocketship
to land in a deserted Kansas field. As a child he knew he
had to move, had to get up from that crash-landed
rocketship and walk all night, across endless cornfields,
until he found the one single house with a porch light
on, walking up to it and, in a child's voice, saying: *Save
me.* We are always leaving worlds behind.

3

Quaker State Oil, Arizona. Edward Weston. Photograph
shown at the Museum of Modern Art (MoMA) as part
of the exhibit *Influences: Walker Evans and Co.* A sign for
the Quaker State Oil company sits off the road, the ex-
panse of sky and a single gray cloud overhead. Nothing
moves. The grayness, stillness, and emptiness over-
whelm the photograph. Nothing changes, as if transformation is impossible here.

4

In the city, if you are relatively young, if you are relatively desperate, every day is filled with an overwhelm-

ing desire to break through—to where an afterthought. Every day the desire to be more burns inside you, and at what cost becomes irrelevant, obscured like some legend of Robert Johnson wrestling the devil at the crossroads. Movement is all that matters, movement like the starsailor, wind in his hair, husks of everything else left behind. The singer Gram Parsons was so beautiful the Rolling Stones wrote the song *Wild Horses* about him. His own songwriting was eerily prophetic, as in *In My Hour of Darkness*, which foretells the shortened life of a traveling singer who visits for a day, leaving only his memory behind with the listener. His bond with his collaborator Emmylou Harris was not physical, but even more intense, and after his messy overdose death—his body stolen from the airport by his buddies, then set on fire in the Joshua Tree desert per the singer's wishes to go out in a blaze of glory and fire and ashes—after such great loss—after lovers, brothers, fathers, planets, and all else disappear—after the realization that you could not save them—after you inherit someone else's dreams—what is there left to do but to carry on, and sing the songs of the dead, guiding them and their words into the mythopoetic cosmic american landscape that endures everlasting. And so many years later, after the man is gone, the songs of devils and grievous angels, of an ill-fated wedding party that becomes a funeral of sorts, of lonely winds and survivors and casualties, songs that break down the barriers between genres and definitions as they break your heart— survive. Transformed—changed—but still alive. We will be remembered always for what we leave behind.

5

During my first years in the city I was always hungry, always eager to attend lectures, readings, museum exhibits, as if what was missing and could fill me might be found there. One night I was part of the audience of a sparsely-attended book event showcasing a translator. He was an elderly white-haired gentleman whose reputation was based solely on his translations into English of the writings of his father, the renown and legendary novelist N. The translator spoke poorly, mumbling and going off on tangents, and very early into his talk he lost the audience, who had begun conversing among themselves, making the reader nearly inaudible. I was able to pick up only bits and pieces of the stories the translator told; one of them seemed to be the tale of the unforgettable night when his father stepped into his bedroom and asked him, then a very young man, to become his translator. Stunned and overwhelmed, the son said *Yes*. I was left wondering about that mythic night: was it a moment strangely wonderful, or beautifully tragic? Was it a fairy tale transformation, the son given wings to fly, or did he become a butterfly caught in a net? In that moment, did N. predestine his son to grow up into one of his own literary characters: the oddball academic, ridiculed behind his back, constantly neurotic, always a tragic figure, the translator known only for being the translator of his father and always cursed to live under that shadow? As I wrestled with these questions, I was drawn into another story the translator was attempting to tell. I'm almost certain I must have misheard it, but what I believe he said was this: that late in his life N. took his son, now a grown man, on a trip up into the mountains. During the day something terrible and strange happened, and someone lost their life. Later that night, the two of them alone, the father became oddly forthcoming and began speaking to his son about his writing. N. said that he was at the end of his writing life. The son recalled his father saying on that strange night in the mountains that writing was like pieces of undeveloped film: the writer's job is to develop the pictures. And he remembers his father, N., saying he had very few pieces of film left.

6

Perhaps it was a problem of mistranslation, perhaps I horribly misheard, but what I recall the translator saying next was that years after the trip, after his father N.'s death, the son found among the father's possessions many pages of unfinished writing. The pages, he believed, were pages of undeveloped film, the pictures unclear, and so the son, the translator entrusted with his father's legacy, says he found within himself the courage to take his father's last pieces of unpublished writing and burn them. And this, in turn, made me think of a great movie that is screened only once, a filmmaker who creates the final masterpiece of his life, and then at its first and only screening the film burning at the same time the images are projected onto the screen, the audience witnessing a movie that will play once and only once, burned forever into their eyes and minds.

7

For a time my hero the starsailor left his adopted planet, tired of it all, perhaps—like N.—thinking that he had come to the end of something. He roamed the planets like Saint-Exupéry's star-traveling prince, with no directions for home. He'd go to sleep on some asteroid, looking out towards the world he left, before going to sleep saying *Goodnight earth, goodnight sun, goodnight city at night like a million lightning bugs in a glass jar. Goodnight.* He had odd dreams, stories with layers like novels, awakening unable to remember stuff about crises of red skies, doomsday battles, and myths of bottled cities. While in exile he missed his job as a reviewer of books and film and music, for he had immersed himself in the pop culture of his adopted planet as only an alien could—with an intensity like religious fervor. In his head he sung to himself the lyrics of a Neil Young song about cold lonely towns in North Ontario where a person's best changes happen. During the day he'd go wandering, coming across people in need of his help on distant planets, involving himself in some planet's seven hundred year wars, and through and through, he'd do the best he could to help those in need, saving every one he could, never resting until all were found—and saved—each and every last one. He'd hold onto them, keep them from falling, battling the winds of space's gravity. It was something he had learned while living in the city—how to hold on as everything falls away from you.

8

Triptych including *Embroidering Earth's Mantle*. Remedios Varo. Paintings shown at the Metropolitan Museum of Art as part of the exhibit *Surrealism: Desire Unbound*. In the first painting, *Toward the Tower*, seven identical-looking girls, each wearing collared Catholic uniforms, ride in a bicycle cavalcade led by their harsh headmistress. Each girl stares hypnotically ahead, spirit broken, while being led to the tall golden tower that will contain her—all save one. One girl has her gaze averted, alert to a black bird flying by her, her eyes bright and free, plans running in her head. In *Embroidering Earth's Mantle*, the next painting, the girls are shown inside the golden tower, each assigned a workstation and watched over by guards as they spend the days sewing. The guards wait impatiently, like seven brothers waiting for their sister to save them. The work of each girl flows forth from small windows cut into the tower imprisoning them, and becomes the very fabric of the world. Amid the seriousness of this scene, one girl, the one with the free gaze from the first painting, allows herself a sly grin, a small sense of satisfaction for the scheme she has put into motion. She has secretly knitted the idea of her freedom, stitching an image of a girl and her lover fleeing the tower into the fabric of her work. An image sewed becomes the sowed seed of *The Escape*, the final image in the triptych, where the girl and her lover are shown fleeing to the mountains. An instance of free thought in the first painting is transformed in the second into a hope of escape that is finally transformed into reality in the final painting. The only way to create the future is to believe in it from the beginning.

9

Being in a city housing the world's greatest museums, every Friday, after a long week's work, I stood in line with others who couldn't afford the regular cost of admission for an opportunity to view the masterpieces on display during each museum's weekly free hours. Crowded with the masses before the artwork on exhibit, I'd wonder if I could ever contribute anything as lasting; I'd wonder if these works were cheapened during these hours opened to the public, whether they shone brighter during regular hours; I'd wonder whether I deserved to be there, to have my gaze on these works; I'd wonder what price each artist paid to achieve their success. My engagement with art would always be touched by these questions. In one museum, large glass windows on an upper floor looked out on a grand old apartment building next door. Through open windows I saw a life I would never have, filled with furniture and lamps and furnishings I didn't know the words for, a quiet wealth that could not be named. So much of living in the city was about yearning for impossible things. The city was always throwing glimpses of distant lands at you—being there made you want so much more of what you couldn't have. So much of my years had been spent dreaming until I was hollow inside, feeling as if I'd given everything away . . . selling one's soul not for change but for less, for just the promise of change . . . and the change was never good enough. All my life I've known there would be a cost for transformation—known it through my sister and brothers and what happened to us. What was the price? A sister's silence, brothers flown away. Some have said that the magician's spell was my fault, the dreamy one, who always wanted so much more; they say I tempted it to happen, desiring the opportunity to fly away. There is nothing as tempting as the hunger of wanting more than is possible, and nothing as dangerous as the movement towards making it happen: in fairy tales they call it *wishing*. In my time exploring the city's museums, the real lesson—the true exhibit—was in glimpsing something I could never have. We spend all our lives preparing to pay the price.

10

STARSAILOR. A picture book in the classic 32-page style. Composed of end pages (pgs. 1 and 32), title spread (pgs. 2-3), and 14 story spreads (pgs. 4-31). *END PAGES: full pages of lithium blue, blue like the sky, collaged to have substance like the snow in Ezra Jack Keats'* The Snowy

Day. *TITLE SPREAD: title all caps in the italic of the Cochin font. Same art to be used in Spread 9: the city, a view from overhead of a crowd during rush hour, within the crowd our hero, mild-mannered, wearing thick geek-chic nerdy-cool black glasses, the starsailor in his civilian identity as a reviewer. Tall buildings all around, all lit up at night.* SPREAD *1*: **The starsailor was a little boy before he became a hero, coming from far away.** *(A rocketship flying through space; through the window a little boy sleeping inside.)* SPREAD *2*: **His rocketship crashed in a cornfield.** *(Rocketship falling into tall corn stalks.)* SPREAD *3*: **When he grew up, he went up into the stars, searching for his home . . .** *(Starsailor, now grown, flying into space; he carries a knapsack on a stick, inside we can sort of see pb&j sandwiches, boxes of fruit juice, apples, etc.)* SPREAD *4*: **. . . but he couldn't find it.** *(Starsailor in empty space, sad look on his face, a single tear.)* SPREAD *5*: **While in space he had fun, surfing on asteroids . . .** *(Use Kirby's Silver Surfer as reference.)* SPREAD *6*: **. . . flying a kite of seven red ravens . . .** *(He is pulled through space by the birds, holding onto strings held in each raven's beak.)* SPREAD *7*: **. . . and riding space horses that sparkled like bright stars.** *(Starsailor riding a horse, wearing a cowboy hat and sunglasses because the horse is so bright.)* SPREAD *8*: **But soon he became lonely, missing his friends, his parents, his city. "Goodnight earth, goodnight sun . . . "** *(Sitting with knees crossed and looking sad on an asteroid, looking out to earth.)* SPREAD *9*: **"Goodnight city at night like a million lightning bugs in a glass jar. Goodnight."** *(See art specs for the title spread: city crowd scene at night with the* *starsailor in his civilian identity, surrounded by tall, lit-up build-ings.)* SPREAD *10*: **He realized, it doesn't matter where you came from, only where you are going. Listen closely, something good is coming, and be prepared to receive it—something great can happen, if only you believe in it.** *(Spread of beautiful stars in space.)* SPREAD *11*: *(Silent spread: crash-landed rocket-ship on fire, hand of little boy reaching out.)* SPREAD *12*: **He flew home, remembering when he was a little boy looking for the answer to a wish.** *(A large corn-field, dwarfing a little boy running through it.)* SPREAD *13*: *(Silent spread: feet, dirtied and bruised, running across cornfield. Footprints left behind.)* SPREAD *14*: **Then finding it.** ***"For every lost boy, there will always appear an opened door."*** *(A scared little boy standing before a big house, the door opening and the light from inside shining upon the boy.)*

11

Once upon a time I was one of seven brothers, chinese, transformed by magic into seven swans. But in my re-search on the internet I see our story being mistold as the tale of the six swans, and in the end all six end up reunited, our sister successfully sewing the shirts to change the brothers back. Our uncle, the goblin king responsible for our transformation, is caught and pun-ished, our sister who suffered years in silence finally able to name our enemy, who is tied to the stake and burned to ashes. All six brothers and the sister finally live together again, happily ever after. I am the seventh brother, the one who wandered off, lost from the tale. I'm the one who ended up in the city, where every day I'm free to begin my story anew. Somewhere in my closet is a pouch of black feathers, and hanging between my cashmere sweaters and suede jackets is a half-finished hand-stitched shirt, reminders of a magic I cannot escape. The feathers and shirt speak of what might have been, like the possibilities on the shelves of the library of lost books in my dreams. In the library of lost books, every book ever written sits on the shelves, every book ever dreamed, even the poems and stories of those who gave up hope and never finished. When you dream yourself there, wanting to sit and read for a while, you might wake up before ever finding that book you're looking for. The rows of shelves stretch for miles and up endless floors, filled with small books and big books, books with spines made of leather and cloth, silver and human skin and butterfly wings, covers stamped with gold and blood and writers' dreams. Every sentence of every book has meaning, each word is committed with hope.

12

Years pass and we find we are not yet transformed to stone, we are still alive. How long has it been, sister? You wear a mask for long enough and you become it. When does wandering transform you into a wanderer? When is a ship no longer a vessel but an empty husk, no further dreams of travel and change sunburned into sea-soaked wood, afloat in silent space with the bones of red ravens bleached white by starlight. Hungry sparkle-horses are roaming and feeding on the edges of our lives. Where have you been, my sister? I have not seen you for so many years. Have you seen the other brothers—the eldest one, with the silver feathers, or the second oldest, with the impenetrable black eyes—the one with the broken wing, and the one who loved to sing at night—and the two twins, born in January, the two who were inseparable. I fear we may have lost them: I last saw them battered by the storm above the Ganges, their coats drenched with rain, one fallen and drowning in the holy river. But don't worry, because I who share a birthday with the day of Lazarus will wander the earth for eternity to tell our story. I have heard that our tormentor was burned to ashes—I think some of those ashes may have flown here, to the city, where they sit on my windowsill, blackened remains of people I do not know that I cannot bring myself to sweep clean as we move through this terrible strange winter.

13

Lost in a Cavern. Henry Darger. Painting shown at the American Folk Art Museum as part of the exhibit *Darger: The Henry Darger Collection of the American Folk Art Museum.* My favorite painting by the outsider artist Darger, whose paintings are usually full of motion and fear, endless running. The recluse who put to canvas his vision of an epic war, his heroines the band of blonde-haired sisters known as the Vivian Girls who face death and slaughter in the paintings and also in Darger's massive unpublished novel, *In the Realms of the Unreal One*, the longest novel ever written. In *Lost in a Cavern* the Vivian Girls are depicted as black silhouettes, their backs turned. They are stranded within a dark cavern, the sky—so present in most Darger paintings—lost to them, the only light entering in the form of a colorful landscape just outside an opening in the cavern. It is a promising mystery: is this an escape into a warless peaceful parallel dimension, or a return to the slaughter fields of the Glandeco-Angelinnean Wars? What life lay beyond that entrance of low-hanging stalactites? The scene is infused with the longing for escape, with the energy from the moment about to happen next. There is a magic there in that moment, a hope that there is more to learn from the darkness than just a legacy of ashes, more than burned pages, more than a body burning in the desert, more than the dust of an exploded planet. There is a magic there that might save you, that might raise you above the drowning waters, beyond a momentary lapse in hope, beyond Paul Celan and his darkest hour, beyond the demons biting at your back.

14

In Los Angeles I attended school a few blocks from the house where two of the Charles Manson murders were committed. All my life that house has haunted me. All my life I've had nightmares about it, only recently beginning to understand the exact details—that there were two sets of murders, that the house we passed on the way to school was the second house, not the first one on Cielo Drive. I have six brothers who also walked by that house every day, without giving it a second thought. Why am I the only one to be so haunted? Years pass and one day you see one of the seminal bands of your youth on T.V. thanking god for the gray hairs in their mohawks. You spend the days searching for a person or place or idea that will make every mushy dumb pop song you ever loved mean something, longing to have bright shining moments instead of another year of unfulfilled dreams. And if you can't achieve that, than maybe the movement towards it—the wishing—is enough for now. Maybe the movement towards the dream will be enough to save you.

15

As a kid, I never got tired of watching cartoons of Gumby and Pokey entering into books, actually stretching and transforming themselves to literally enter inside a book in their library and to have adventures between the covers. Books were alive, and within them were infinite possibilities. In my earliest book memory, I remember a used book fair in Chinatown where old discarded library books were being sold off. My father, who usually never wanted to buy us anything, insisted that I pick out a book, and somewhat randomly I chose a hardcover storybook, the dust jacket missing, about a little ghost. In the story, the family the ghost had haunted had moved away, and the lonely lost ghost was searching for a place where he belonged. The little ghost's story was tragic, his despair mixed with an innocent hope for possibility, a nagging belief that something better was out there, something good was waiting. There was something so raw and personal in that story, I can't help being touched by it as I try to write my own. When I was younger I felt the fairy tale forces around me, their power, and later, even scarier, I began feeling my own power to shape my world, transformed by loss but able to make something from the ashes. No one knows how my story will end, whether the story will be heard, or compromised, or silenced, or become lost in that library of lost books. So many things have happened, so much time has passed since the story began, but of all the books in the library of lost books, I know the one that I'd always want is my own.

MYSTERY BOY

ven as a young boy I saw my future as a teen detective. And so I fooled myself into believing it
was my destiny to find clues written in the sand,
hidden meanings in a curve in the road, my fate to one
day lose myself in cases like *The Secret of the Chinese Boat*,
sailing out into dark harbors and discovering flashing
mystery lights, looking out across the slowly-crashing
waves and seeing my future and my past reflected there
in the water. Solving mysteries became an addiction,
the mystery life a drug I couldn't kick. Those youth
mysteries were like heroin: once hooked, we were detectives for life, always chasing the dragon, never able to
leave that world where clues arrived unannounced and
strangers were always hidden in shadows. The end of
each mystery was never enough, because as soon as one
case was over another arrived in the form of a note in
an old clock, a map inscribed into a tree, a manuscript
in a stone garden, a key hidden beneath dead leaves.

Accompanying more seasoned sleuths on cases, I would always be struck by a sense of *jamais vu*: the feeling of not having experienced a place or action before but knowing I should have. The whole *Secret of the Chinese Boat* case was like that, like being drowned in an unlived history that should have been familiar and recognizable, because that was why I was there in the first place—to find special meaning in old Chinese proverbs like *Boat with no eyes cannot see!*, to locate hidden clues on our dragon boat of eyes and scales, to outsmart all the strange Chinese men suddenly popping out of the woodwork all over Bayside. *Good grief, another one?* Chet muttered, seeing the man we would know as Tzi Ming approaching our docked boat, the *Golden Promise*. He was dapperly dressed in a white summer suit and straw hat, and he'd come here to persuade us boy sleuths to sell our mystery boat for a generous sum and, when politely refused, to offer a barely-veiled threat: *There is an old Chinese saying that bad luck follows those who will not be reasonable*, Tzi Ming warned, his eyes slitted with annoyance. Again with the old sayings, I said to myself, wanting to rewrite my life as a blank slate, my history disappearing like rain falling into the ocean. There was a mystery surrounding our boat, something about it that all the suspects like fisherman Dags Chowder, Tzi Ming, and all the other Chinese men desperately wanted—this much was as clear as water. The first time our boat was tampered with, we had a full boatload of passengers and a hole cut into the bottom of the *Golden Promise*, the work of saboteurs for sure. With buckets and fast hands, we worked frantically to prevent the boat from sinking before we could steer ourselves back to the safety of the pier in Bayside. More trouble followed, and the second time we faced danger out at sea we boy sleuths were alone, far out in the fog-drenched waters when our engine suddenly and mysteriously quit. It was an eerie sensation, lying still on the water, cut off from the outside world. We took turns ringing the junk's bell to signal for help, and from time to time muffled sounds drifted through the swirling mist. Adrift, surrounded by fog, we could see no sign of land and it was easy to pretend we were the last boy detectives on earth. Peering over the railing, all we could make out was the lapping of waves alongside the stalled boat, and white foam, kelp, and occasionally disks of perfectly clear water, like perfect circles of eternity passing by. Frank said they looked like whale prints, footprints left behind in the ocean by whales when they surfaced near the top of the water to exhale and breathe, and that seemed as good an explanation as any to that mystery. I remembered public school field trips in Los Angeles, when our class would ride a school bus down to San Pedro Harbor to go whale watching, spotting humpback gray whales out on the Pacific Ocean, returning to school with stories of seeing the Love Boat sailing away and the cast of *CHiPs* filming nearby, Erik Estrada and his publicist stepping aboard for a moment to greet us inner city school children and hand out autographed photos. And although the magic of that day would not last, as if everything Ponch must eventually fade away, we were left touched by the memory of that moment and its infinite possibilities, possibilities I've been searching for throughout all my mysteries: perfect solutions and days so ferociously full of grace, not mysteries filled with *déjà vu* or *jamais vu* or any feelings equally frenchy and not adding up, but the kind of mystery where the ominous letter found tucked in the old clock that chimes once every hour reads *A great day lies ahead in the not too distant future*, and you can believe it. Floating out in the fog by Rockaway Isle, anchorless and receiving no reply to our calls for help, we seemed lost in time and could imagine any of our fellow sleuths appearing out of the thick mists to save us, even those we'd failed to save. There were so many ghosts of the past, like Billy Wild and the Grace Sisters and Matthew Fate, and also ghosts of the present and future, those we knew would be casualties of the mysteries like the Lucky Wongs, victims of an unsolved plane crash, and the Arson Twins, two brilliant mute sisters in jail, and Dave Fearless, the Trouble Twins, Tommy Tomorrow. Like my idol Daniel Hope and like so many before them, out of the wreckage of their lives they built some small bit of grace. Daniel Hope was my role model, despite being only a couple of years older than me and the Hardwick Boys, the kind of sleuth I've always tried to emulate. He became a detective despite abandonment by his parents and a childhood spent in orphanages and foster homes but, like too many of us, lost the game of chasing the dragon, losing himself in quiet despair and rage to become another casualty of the mysteries. I wanted so much to be just like him, but without the anger, and without the desperation. I was still looking for something in the mysteries that could save me. And so we return to the moment I first stepped onto the *Golden Promise*: *Welcome aboard, honored guest,* Joe said solemnly, bowing low in an Oriental manner, and being a good-humored Chinese American lad I chuckled and responded: *Boy, that's corny enough for a Grade D movie about China!* And then we found the cuff link of rare blue amber, which must have fallen from a masked suspect during a struggle on the boat's deck. We later found another blue amber cuff link, the twin to the first one, outside a cave in the woods, lying in the dirt alongside a trail of footprints that we followed until they connected with tire marks and then faded out altogether. Somehow I knew that blue amber was called "tiger soul" in old Chinese legends, that it was believed that when a tiger died, its spirit penetrated the earth and turned to amber. The mystery life transformed our souls, too; living through it made us hard as rock inside, living statues of boy and girl detectives. Looking out across the water as we were finally towed back to shore by a coast guard boat, I knew I didn't want to be so hard and angry just to get through this life, I didn't want to always be in need of rescue. Tony Primo was waiting for us on the pier as lightning flashed in the sky and from underneath shelter he called out to us: *Hurry, fellas! The sky's going to fall any second.*

·   ·   ·

The first time I met Frank and Joe Hardwick I was a body buried in leaves, a corpse lying in Dead Men's Forest. I was pretending to be dead, covered in a layer of dried leaves while their buddies Tommy, Nina, Chet, and Nancy led them to the scene of their discovery. Joe reached down and touched my face, brushing the dead leaves from my closed eyes, and as he did so I opened my eyes and smiled. I rose from that ocean of leaves and that was the beginning of the mysteries. From then on I was an occasional sleuth, the trusted partner when the going got tough; I saw the world that full-time boy detectives like Frank and Joe saw every day, and I became a part of that. Like them, I began to see clues everywhere: mysterious colored bubbles in the summer air, messages written in the sand, footprints heading east, then disappearing in the haunted forest, strange bright lights in the night sky. It was these sort of mystery lights that our pals Biff Hoover and Tony Primo spotted during *The Secret of the Chinese Boat*, confirming the strange old beachcomber Dags Chowder's contention of seeing lights over Rockaway Isle. *We saw them, too—they were blinking on and off, as if someone was sending a message in secret code!* Tony revealed in an excited voice. So one rainy night we boys slept aboard our boat the *Golden Promise*, taking turns watching and waiting for the lights to appear. *Wow!* Joe cried out, startling the rest of us awake. *There they are. Let's get going, fellows! Now's our chance to find out who's sending secret signals from Rockaway Isle!* I was assigned the task of guarding the boat, watching as my friends rushed blindly out into the rain toward the end of the wet pier where a group of masked men jumped out of the shadows and confronted them. My fear for them was short-lived, because just then I heard lightning overhead. For a moment, I was on fire. *The Golden Promise has been hit!!!* I heard someone scream in the distance. I was burning. After what happened, I would recall the day the mysterious Chinese man Chow Lew appeared at the Hardwicks' home, stating that he represented a religious group in China who wanted to buy the *Golden Promise* because it was a sacred boat of theological and historical importance. As we pondered the idea, just then the telephone rang; Frank answered it and looked at us excitedly. *Wow! Wait till you guys hear this!!* he whispered. It was a telegram from Tzi Ming, one of the other strange Chinese men wanting our boat, saying: *DON'T SELL THE HAI HUA AT ANY PRICE OR THE CURSE IT CARRIES WILL DESCEND UPON YOU.* So our boat was either blessed or cursed, and we didn't know which story to believe. After being struck by lightning, I began to believe both were true: I was hit by lightning and set on fire, but I survived. One of the boat's dragon eyes took the brunt of the hit—the lightning destroyed it and burned the jacket I was wearing. But I escaped disaster, one of those people about whom they could say: *And he walked away. He lived to tell the tale.* And by joining the cult of boy detectives, I was trying to walk away from a past, to rewrite a life. Bayside and the Los Angeles I came from—it was a tale of two cities. That Los Angeles was not how it is today, remade by retroactive continuity into trendy Silver Lake, a place of tattooed and body-pierced artists. Back then, it was a place you wouldn't want so permanently carved into yourself—it existed only to be escaped. All my life I've tried to rewrite myself, looking for the tools to make it happen—I was Jan Brady searching for a typewriter that dropped its *y*'s, a boy detective searching for the source that produced a typewritten clue. In the *Chinese Boat* case we received just such a note. For a while we suspected Dags Chowder, the weird old fisherman who haunted the bay, and we even broke into his house while Chet distracted him to check his typewriter. What we found was a house full of junk: piles of notes and books stacked high, stacks of old magazines covering the floor, a museum of items salvaged while beach-combing—a boat anchor with a broken fluke, numer-ous carvings of driftwood, coils of hemp line—and, sitting atop an old orange crate, an old typewriter that most definitely didn't match the one we were looking for. The odd house was bursting with an old man's weird imagination—the books and magazines revealed the old kook was a voracious reader, and stranger yet, the piles of pages stacked next to his typewriter re-vealed that he was writing what appeared to be a Tom Clancy-type novel. I read a section: it was about a man living near the beach, confronted by government con-spiracy mysteries and butting heads with a band of know-it-all kids who were apparently clueless about the scope of the web of espionage and intrigue sur-rounding their little world; the man was depicted as not perfect, just an average joe trying to keep sane in an insane world. Like the protagonist of that book, I was trying to keep my head above it all, even when I knew all along—whether underwater or buried beneath leaves—I was always close to drowning.

As future detectives we stood out from other children growing up. We were the ones who went to school with black fingerprint dust staining our hands, the ones drowsy from nights spent looking over clues. We were the children who never met a corpse we didn't find interesting, the ones other children hated because we had to know all the answers. Somehow we knew we were heading someplace with our overactive curiosity, even if we didn't know for sure where. We were *Becoming X*, we told ourselves, and someday we would know what that meant. Then came the day when we were rewarded. One by one we were blindfolded and led down steps. When we could see once again, we found ourselves in a smoky room of dim lights—it smelled like magic. We took the pledge of the secret society of teen sleuths, learned the secret codes and signals, memorized sacred oaths and rituals. We received a special spyglass and were schooled in all the secret handshakes. We would place our coven of mystery solvers above all else: our government, God, and family. *X* became known: we were true detectives at last. Our fingers were pricked and our blood smeared on a photo of Diana Wise, one of the first teen detectives to die in service, fallen during *The Mystery in the Hidden Woods*. We held the photo of the girl sleuth in our hands and it was set on fire. We were changed from that moment on, our earlier ordinary lives now buried and forgotten like a relic of the past. We left that life like a burning building.

Once upon a time, I was a boy detective. I was the sidekick and occasional partner to a boy sleuth or two, a helpful chum when the going got tough, a trusted assistant on difficult cases, helping to locate the hidden treasure, to translate the found documents written in a foreign language, to decode the mysterious map, to unriddle the obscure clue left behind. And to be there, when the mystery turned, to run for your life, to scatter in all directions, chased across the icy cold lakes of Rockaway Isle, through the dark caves on top of Signal Hill, and across the hidden trails of Dead Men's Forest, tangled vines around our feet.

And if we tripped up now and again, everything would eventually turn out all right in the end. Angels watched over us. We'd close the case, the mystery revealed and ourselves alive. It was a blessed life, while it lasted.

My best-known case was probably *The Secret of the Chinese Boat*, which was solved with Frank and Joe, Biff, Chet, and Tony—my teen sleuth friends from Bayside. That case involved hidden treasures, extortion, medical fraud, hostage taking, and a mysterious international jewel thief known as the Chameleon, a master of disguise. All of these elements were tied somehow to the boat in the case's title, a junket called the *Hai Hau*, Chinese for *Golden Promise*. This was the key case in my career as a teen detective, and I remember, after the case was over, sitting alone for a moment on the bow of the *Golden Promise*, looking out over the water and remembering the danger, the thrills, the triumphant ending where everything was set so right, justice over evil and all that, the case of *The Secret of the Chinese Boat* solved and closed.

And I wondered: Would the rest of my life live up to the promise of this mystery?

Aboard the boat, dragon eyes stared through me. They were fake and cheap, ornamental designs carved throughout the boat, all bright-colored and gaudy, like the lobby of a bad Chinese restaurant. The ethnic flourishes were a major attraction of the old, used boat, which us boy detectives bought as a group at a bargain to run a summer ferry service and sightseeing business on the waters of local Bayside. When he first saw the gaudy vessel, Frank exclaimed: *Oh boy! This junk may have once belonged to some Chinese pirate and have jade treasure hidden aboard!!*

And it did, of course, in the form of a hidden map leading to mines of rare blue amber in China. The map was what everyone was after, all the scary people we ran across in this case: Chow Lew and his henchmen; another mysterious figure named Tzi Ming; the coastguard impersonators; and Dr. Rosemont, a.k.a. Balarat, the Chameleon. We learned that the co-conspirators were communicating with one another across the waters by sending signals from Rockaway Isle, lights which blinked on and off over the rocks and cliffs, imparting messages in secret code.

Sitting alone onboard the docked boat, I saw that the bay was calm and motionless except for the movement of the tides and a light cool breeze in the air. On the pier, Frank and Joe and the rest of the boys were finishing up their reports to the police, while the criminals had been taken away, to jail or back to China or wherever. I looked out into the darkness of the waters and the huge black sky, and I made a wish that these days would continue forever.

And across the darkness, in answer to my hopes, was a searchlight suddenly gleaming from the western cliffs.

When I rejoined the others on the pier, nobody else mentioned the sign from the cliffs, and I would keep that searchlight secret, a hidden memory.

I would remember the promise of that night years later, during times when it seemed that unexpected answer had lied—a *red herring*, as we would label misleading clues. That night would come back in bad times, when being lost in the life of a boy detective seemed far too distant and it looked as if I were to be just another casualty of the mysteries.

I'm telling this part now because it leads into the rest of my story—my memoirs of a boy detective—and how I found myself becoming a sleuth again: this was the beginning of things.

.   .   .

Once upon a time, I died as a child.

This was in Los Angeles, in the second grade, and it was announced to me at recess on the playground during the first day of school. It had been on the news over the summer, the murder of another child with my name. Thinking it was me, my classmates and teachers were really surprised to see me alive and beginning a new school year.

I was famous for a short time because of my murdered namesake, my brother in name, but eventually everyone stopped talking about it, that murder of myself that almost happened. It was not the child they knew but another one: an anonymous murder they couldn't relate to. Everyone forgot about it except for me, who realized that my almost-death was one of the few ways someone from my school would get on the evening news. It was not the world of boy detectives who solved crimes and were lauded with ribbons and knickknacks. It was a place of limited possibilities for children to achieve fame: a child murdered, a child missing, a child saved from near-death.

So becoming a boy detective was the greatest magic trick of all time, like pulling a new life out of a hat, creating a world of opportunity and meaning from thin air. Finding myself in Bayside solving cases was like discovering magic. And you could say that the role I played in those mysteries was infused with a sense of the magical: I was the chinese mystic, the guardian of superstitions, the bearer of fortune cookies. In *The Secret of the Chinese Boat* I was the translator, the tour guide, the informing native. I explained customs and superstitions that I only knew second-hand if at all, and I translated found clues, street signs, and menus.

That clue-like messages could be found in fortune cookies amazed some of the boy sleuths:

Yikes! Why, there's a funny little paper inside my cookie?! exclaimed Chet, the plump youth having just bitten into one of the crispy cookies served after our delicious Chinese dinner. We were rewarding ourselves after an especially brilliant and magical day, when all the clues had come together perfectly and we seemed on the brink of cracking the case.

Read it, Chet, if you want to see your future, I said, a sly grin on my face.

Biff, Frank, Joe, and the others had already read their own fortunes. GREAT WEALTH IS IN YOUR FUTURE, read Frank's fortune, predicting the end of our mystery.

Joe's fortune said BEWARE THE WORLD SPLITTING INTO TWO. It was a warning about the future, I realize now, but back then, we just expressed a sigh of bemused puzzlement.

Then all eyes turned to Chet, awaiting the reading of his fortune. Chet appeared indignant, staring angrily and chagrined at his tiny piece of paper. *Huh!? Mine says,* WARNING! YOU SHOULD GO ON A DIET!

The rest of us burst out laughing!! Between guffaws, Frank warned, with mock seriousness, *Better not finish that cookie, Chet.*

You guys just don't understand, the stout boy exclaimed. *I just need lots of food energy for all the work I do!!!*

We all responded to Chet's indignation with fresh merriment. Later, to prove his boast, Chet attempted to balance himself along the bowline of the *Hai Hau*, with the expected result of falling headfirst into the cold water. Biff and Frank jumped in immediately to rescue him, dragging Chet to the shore where, sputtering and crying, he apologized profusely for all the trouble his antics caused. He almost drowned on the shore from his own tears and snot, his face red and embarrassed, the earlier magic of the day now entirely gone.

That day would seem to foretell all our futures: brightness early on, followed by times to come when we would all need to be saved from drowning.

But during the brightness, when we were "on," we forgot the warnings of the future; fortune cookie messages were carelessly lost and thrown out. My own fortune from that night read BE CAREFUL WHAT YOU BELIEVE IN, but I ignored it, tossing it into the water of the bay that same night.

The solutions to many of our cases proved that chance, fate, and time work in odd ways. Sometimes clues just appeared to us, impossibly, unbelievably, without any sense of logic or reality at all. A message written in the sand, a note taped to the face of a clock, a key discovered in a shell—clues laid out for bright children for whom the world was their oyster.

Similarly, it seems, the future appears to others: in fortune cookies, in visions, and in dreams. On T.V., I've seen a woman whose dreams foretell the end of the planet. America as we know it no longer exists in this heartland housewife's nightly visions, where she sees five maps of a whole new world.

Perhaps this apocalyptic future is our true reality, and the rest of us are dreaming, asleep and unaware of the lost prophets buried deep in America, the mystics waiting only to be discovered. We are all lost in dreamland, lost in the fiction of children's stories, trapped in the Area 51 of our minds. We live as slaves to speculation, nostalgia, and sweet mystery.

If this were so, I would give myself totally to it. I would believe entirely in the alien autopsy film of my life as a boy detective.

I built a life.

No hoax, no imaginary story, no what ifs.

I made myself into the kind of boy who could be a boy detective, the type of child finding clues alongside the likes of the world's most famous teen sleuths, and not the type of boy who would *be* the clue—the corpse found, the body missing, the life murdered. I was the magician behind the most important act of my life.

Somewhere out there is a parallel me who I've murdered: plain, poor, average. I have eradicated one possible life—my existence before Bayside, the child who would have grown up dull and graceless, without adventure, or opportunity, or mystery.

All across the land, as future detectives go to sleep, they imagine clues, puzzles, solutions, weird objects that they must decipher. They dream the life they plan to make a reality. They hope: let me live a long life full of mysteries.

And they pray: *Oh god, let it not be normal.*

• • •

The mysteries were what saved me, saved me from days of ordinariness and boredom, from a half-life, a life filled with days of maybe-next-year. The mysteries gave me an identity, rescuing me from anonymity.

They served a role in my childhood like saints and angels do for other children, children in places like Lourdes and Bosnia and Rwanda.

These children, they go to the grotto, to the grove, to the cave, to the wooded path—they go to these places to meet up with miracles.

They go to these places to find a saint or the Virgin Mary, and they return again and again, even if the visions will not appear, because it is their destiny.

The children return to the grotto, to the grove, to the cave because they are places of possibility, an alternate world revealed to them when reality sucks.

All my life I've wanted so badly the power to split into two different people: the person before and the person after, the old self and the new, like Norma Jean and Marilyn, or a boy without hope and a boy detective— and, now, a detective guy at the end of the mysteries and just a regular guy with hope.

All my life I've always wanted so much more than what I had, and eventually I learned that the mysteries alone were not enough—the person after a mystery ended was too much like the person before.

• • •

I attended the school of detectives, but there were many others, equally talented, who never had that chance. These were the ones who just missed being detectives for life, the ones who escaped the power of the mysteries. These others: they were the detectives who would never be.

A detective who specialized in cases of lost pets, who would eventually retire and attend dental school. Detectives solving mysteries of expired food, lost keys, missing change, misdirected mail. One who investigated Pink Floyd's *Dark Side of the Moon* album and the mystery behind its strange synchronicity to particular movies. In time their sleuthing powers would disappear and they would go on with their lives. Another who solved mysteries of strangers you sat next to on planes and trains—people who touch your life briefly who you may think of every few years, recalling snippets of conversation. Whatever happened to them? These were mysteries for the girl sleuth of strangers met in public places.

And others of the detectives who never were: the boy detective of unrequited teen crushes, the sleuth of failed poets, the girl investigator of department store sales, the teenage private eye of items washed-up on the beach. In their own way, they were teen sleuths as well.

And I'd imagine them saving us, using the methods that were their own—the answers locked within their own mysteries, solutions buried along trails of wet dreams and broken hearts, hidden in bad poetry only to be found in back issues of *Ploughshares*, the *Beloit Fiction Journal*, and the *Chatahoochee Review*, secret clues encoded among the red tag sale labels at Nordstroms, Macy's, and Banana Republic, the answer waiting to be washed up on the beach, uncovered there among sea shells and seaweed, the clue that would save us all.

We are a dying breed. Our detective tribe is dwindling, heading into the new millennium with our numbers growing smaller each year. One day we will be gone entirely—a time will come when all that remains are hidden clues to our previous existence, vestiges like the clues to those fifty-year-old, hundred-year-old mysteries we'd encounter: unsolved cases reappearing by chance in times when no one is left to care about the solution. There was a spookiness to those cases—each a mystery with only a center and nothing else to it, all meaning grown old and brittle, the value of finding a solution lost. Seventy-five-year-old unsolved child murders, where the child if alive would be no more, having disappeared into grizzled old age.

Our imminent extinction is inevitable, according to figures compiled by Marshall Brady, librarian boy detective and archivist for the group. The active teen detective population, which includes those of us in our twenties and thirties who remain alive, has shown a steady decrease since the 1980s, with projected figures for the new millennium showing this trend continuing.

Like animals, we are dying out.

In my youth, there was an ebb and flow to life like the graphs and charts that now mark our decline. We knew we were not the first, and we would not be the last. On every adventure we'd discover some new sleuth, a new friend with his or her own special gimmicks and ways of solving cases. Now the idea of the last teen detective on earth is not so incredible. The last detective searching for uneasy answers, investigating the final clues left behind by the last of their tribe. One day this last sleuth might dig us up from the ground. Like dinosaurs, all that would remain would be piles of bones in the teen sleuth graveyard.

And maybe that would be the last mystery: the last teen sleuth could lie down and die then and there, the final mystery solved. Our story will have ended, the last of us come home to join us, the millennium's fading light shining on old bones.

I used to believe that before I became a boy detective, I'd been waiting all my life for my destiny to find me. I was simply passing the days, biding time, waiting for that moment to arrive. When it happened, it was like stepping into a dream.

What I couldn't know in those days before I became a boy detective was the danger. I couldn't feel the punches, the slaps and bruises of that life.

So many of the mysteries were about survival— about fighting to live. In my first big case, five of us ended up chained together—Frank and Joe Hardwick, Tommy Tomorrow, Josh Slocum, and myself. We knew our captors would kill us. We didn't give them that chance, using our bodies as a battering ram to knock down an escape route at the rear of the boat where we were held hostage. Then we had to make it to shore. Tied up together in a line, our hands chained behind each of us, we knew it was all or nothing. Either all five of us would escape and be alive, or none of us would. Frank led the way. Chained together we managed to climb onto a small plank at the boat's rear. A light rain made the surface wet and slippery, but we only needed a few seconds to compose ourselves, to find courage and wait for Frank's signal to jump into the dark water below. We could feel each other's fear, hear one another's pounding heartbeats. Bound so close to one another by chains, we knew that one boy sleuth's fear could be passed along from troubled heart to troubled heart. We had to conquer fear. We knew that not one of us could give in to it. *Ready!* Frank yelled, and then he gave the signal for us to leap out into the night, splashing together as one into the freezing water below. We found ourselves under the water, the world dead silent. Then we fought for the surface, kicking with our feet, and we made our way to the nearby dock, arriving underneath it, resting against hard rocks.

This was our intimacy, our closeness. It was ugly, our ways of survival. So many times we found ourselves packed together like sardines, hiding or escaping, the taste of rubber in my mouth, a shoe, an elbow. So many nights I dreamt nightmares of dead boys on top of me, the weight keeping me down.

God—that was one helluva night, we'd say afterwards, alive.

It was amazing how we survived. *Atta boy!* we'd say, heaving a heavy sigh of relief. Then hugs and pats on the back. *Boy, what a night!* And then the reminder: no one else could know, how we barely escaped. Our worries were our own—trouble passed along from one anxious mind to the other, within our brotherhood of sleuths. It was our secret, held tight within the cult of teen detectives.

Whenever I was away from Bayside, my dreams at night were busy ones, filled with trails of footprints, hidden treasure, counterfeiters, ghost ships, and mystery lights. Those dream images were a reminder of things, of how mysteries still existed in Bayside. Those dreams gave me a feeling that boy detectives were still needed— that although we had left the town and gone on with our lives, all the while the mysteries were still alive back there, still smoldering, waiting for our inevitable return.

When we did return, back in town for a case with Joe and the others, the first day of our investigations would be interrupted by our need to pay our respects to those who came before us. There were so many it scared me sometimes, those who had died. The grave of the first teen sleuth to die in service, the beautiful Diana Wise, was marked by an elaborate bronze sculpture of her namesake, the goddess of the hunt. We left flowers for her and remembered our initiations, when a photo of Diana was burned in our hands as we took the oath of boy detectives. Joe went around and pulled weeds from the headstones around the people we had known, sleuths like Matthew Fate, Dave Fearless, and Harry Oliver and Billy Blue, the Trouble Twins. He left flowers on the grave marker for Tommy Tomorrow, whose body we knew was not buried there, but elsewhere. I lit incense on the graves of the Lucky Wongs and left tangerines. I cleaned the headstone of Daniel Hope.

We left bones and chew toys for Togo I and Togo II. Their graves were right next to those of the Grace Sisters—Sarah, Jessica, and Allison, all lying next to one another in a row. All of the gravesites we visited were marked with white crosses.

The dead have always scared me. There were vengeful ghosts, I knew, waiting to carry us over to the other side. They were angry at us for being alive. Josh Slocum—the surfer sleuth—believed it, too. He was fond of saying that anyone who'd spent as much time out alone at sea as he had must have once heard the calls of drowned men, wishing for him to join them, or the siren calls of mermaids, who were really ghosts of the sea.

Along with River View, Bayside was one of the two twin capital cities of sleuthing. Diana Wise had adopted Bayside as her place of operations, as had many others.

Even though they were not originally from Bayside, those detectives came here and found a home, the same way people leave small towns in the Midwest to build new lives in New York or San Francisco and never leave. So many of them, like Diana Wise, became legends, and now they remain here, buried far from their hometowns.

They came from cities with names like Sandytown and Twin Peaks and Sprindrift Island and Star City, places soon bereft of a boy or girl detective.

None of us ever packed up our suitcases and went there, to those places we knew only from a map. None of us ever thought to replace them, after their deaths. None of us who'd survived could hope to replace those legends. We could not carry their torch. They had become too large in our imagination for anyone to fill their shoes.

Bayside was a town always covered in mist and fog. It was a town where so much was hidden, and secrets obscured. Fog floated everywhere, all over the town, all the time, even in summer weather.

To be caressed by fog is not as nice as it might sound. It was unsettling, just like seeing wisps of smoke curling everywhere, creeping behind you like animals. Wearing glasses in Bayside weather was impossible, because they fogged up immediately.

In *The Secrets of the Apple Orchard Keys* we tested out some ultra-violet night goggles for the first time, Joe and I. We had the hardest time, I remembered. We were surveying the apple orchard owned by old Mrs.

Crandall, wearing our night goggles, and not only did we not see any better, we couldn't see at all, the lenses clouded by moisture. We stumbled around blindly, falling like fools and tripping over apples.

In *The Secret of the Chinese Boat*, fog covered us as we were out in the water, the engine of our boat stalled. The fog was so dense we couldn't even peer overboard and see the surface of the water, see what fortunes were written on the face of the waves. The fog was so heavy it made sense why some people used that "pea soup" expression. We thought that if the fog in the air was that thick, then perhaps the water below us would be just as hard, or harder, that we could make our escape by walking across the water back to Bayside, if we could walk on water.

On the best of days in Bayside, the fog and the mist cleared away and the days shone like smuggled coins. Out on the beaches, the combination of clouds, blue, and sun made the sky appear like a 3-D shoebox diorama. The sky took on shape and contour, like a collaged sky in a Henry Darger painting. Behind each layer of sky one could imagine another dimension existing, appearing from behind a curtain of clouds like Brigadoon, appearing on our plane of existence only once every ten years. We could imagine a hint of those other places—a wind of those mysteries blowing through, a mystery from another world. And we longed to go there, where the mysteries were sweeter, longed to enter into that world like smugglers of Pirate's Cove, hidden, undercover.

The weather in Bayside was a powerful phenomenon. It was like a divine force. We were in awe of it as kids.

We were like avatars of the weather, lightning rods for mysteries and all sorts of bad things. Living in the mysteries was like trying to dodge lightning: no matter what safety position you assumed, no matter how hard you tried to hide, you never knew when you'd be hit.

When I was hit by lightning onboard the *Golden Promise*, I thought I had been shot through the heart.

Josh Slocum says that when he was struck by lightning out at sea, he felt his tongue sizzling and popping like frying bacon. He was lucky that his boat floated back to the Bayside dock on its own.

Lightning can strike even when the storm is miles away. When it hits, it is four times hotter than the surface of the sun. People struck have had their hearts stop. For others, it can cause permanent brain damage, or spinal cord injury.

My lightning experience was atypical in that I recovered soon afterwards. Josh's experience was more normal of those who survive: for days afterward, all he could think of was his sudden brush with death. He was typical of those who cannot even talk for days, their thoughts solely focused on the seconds when they were on fire, and when they do speak only one word comes from their mouths. All they can say is *lightning, lightning, lightning, lightning, lightning.*

. . .

If you find yourself trapped outside when lightning hits, you will want to get into the lightning-safe position. This is what you should do to protect yourself. When stuck out in the wide open, the goal is to make yourself as small a target as possible. The safety position resembles the position for earthquakes: you crouch down, on your knees, with your hands over your ears, bent over. Assuming the lightning-safe position is a little like praying.

Being killed by lightning is the leading cause of weather-related death—more common than tornados and hurricanes.

Nina Sorrow—the psychic girl detective—had a roommate in college who had been struck twice by lightning when she was a small girl. She hid in closets and refused to come out when the weather was bad.

Being struck twice was a mixed blessing. Either you're watched over by the angels, to have survived twice, the unlikeliest of miracles, or it was a sign of being one of the unluckiest people on the planet, the odds of being hit two times the worst kind of bad luck.

Being able to walk around and say you've been hit by lightning puts you in a special group—a small, exclusive club of those of us who have been struck by lightning and survived. We go on living, knowing that at any given time there are more than two thousand thunderstorms raging around the world.

. . .

We were all struck by lightning in our youth, those of us living in Bayside.

Somehow chosen by the mysteries, we teen sleuths were caught up in an awesome phenomenon just outside our scope of understanding. It was as electrifying and just as scary as actually being hit by lightning.

There were lots of mysteries out there in Bayside, and they all found us. In time we learned to sense a mystery coming.

When I knew a mystery would soon find me I got a bad feeling in my stomach and wanted to just stay home, indoors, sleeping for twelve hours straight. I'd stay inside watching bad T.V. and eating frozen waffles for dinner until I knew the mystery had my name on it, that I was destined to intercept it—that it was my responsibility, my destination.

I knew a case was coming just like I knew lightning would strike from the buzzing noise, from the electrified air and people's hair floating up. When lightning is about to strike you can literally see it coming down to earth. As it gets closer, the lightning electrifies everything, creating an electric field, and you can see and hear the effects of the field around you.

The worst places to be when lightning strikes are under a tree, or in water. When I was hit I was surrounded by water, on a boat in the bay. Josh Slocum was also out in deep water. It used to be that the majority of people in America hit by lightning were struck while outside at work: the nation's farmers, ranchers, sharecroppers. Nowadays that's no longer true and the most common place to be hit by lightning is a golf course, a testament to the way the world has changed and the nation's long gone agrarian past. You can add that to the list of facts about lightning, with bonus points for the use of the phrase "agrarian past."

Most lightning strikes occur at the beginning or at the end of a storm. Like a mystery, all is not safe until it's finally over. For us boy detectives, though, there was always the next mystery waiting just outside the door.

People have asked me if the lightning affected my brain. Am I terrified every time it rains? I've spoken with Josh about this, and I think for both of us the answer is no. I was mauled by a dog at the age of five, but I still love puppies. When I'm alone at home and it begins to rain, I just lock the doors and shut the windows, and I remind myself that three-fourths of people struck by lightning survive the experience.

In the stories of homunculi, common objects—like bread or dirt—can create a living, breathing thing when mixed together. My grandmother believed in it, thought that the sudden appearance of worms after a rain shower was caused by dirt mixing with rainwater and leaves, the three elements together creating worms when struck by lightning. Lightning was often the catalyst for animating the mix of common objects.

For example:

DUST + YARN + MOSS + LIGHTNING = MICE
RAIN + BREAD + DIRT + LIGHTNING = BIRDS
ROTTEN MEAT + SEMEN + LIGHTNING = CHILDREN

RAGS + WORMS + BLOOD + RAIN + LIGHTNING =
A PATCHWORK MAN

In the course of the mystery life, we too learned some of the formulas that governed the world.

Some cases, though, we could not comprehend, no matter how we broke them down to their basic elements. About a decade ago, for example, we were called to San Diego County to help with a string of suicides. People reported that there was a spirit driving around in a big black van, coming to claim them. They believed they would die, and their anxiety caused their deaths by their own hands. There was nothing we could do in this case. How can you even begin to understand something like that?

The answers were a mystery, just like the equations that governed us, but what were the formulas to our own lives?

When burned at the stake, Joan of Arc was said to have turned into gas and light. I wonder what isotopes we would break down into, us boy and girl detectives? How would we unravel into dirt and bread, wind, water, fire, air?

When we plummeted into the water during our escape in *The Secret of the Chinese Boat,* we hit the water and stayed under for a few seconds, chained together, the five of us boys. We stayed lost underneath that silent wet world. I wanted to remain down there, in that quiet haven, and I could feel the rest of the guys wanting to give in too. It was peaceful. It made us wish we could breathe down there underwater.

We were safe from the world above for a few seconds. The water was a reprieve from the fiasco of the mysteries, back up in the world we knew. We enjoyed that brief time, before we pushed up, all our lives at stake while chained together, before we had to come up for air and abandon our peaceful kingdom.

We returned to the mysteries to watch our lives turn like pages. Still, we always secretly longed for escape—for the freedom we found in places like underneath the water.

Escape meant living free, and living free meant dying in your own time. It meant not being a slave to the clues. It meant that one day the world might open up, no longer a closed book of mysteries, and allow us the sense of safety and joy we never allowed ourselves as kids.

These things happen, and you need to be ready for them.

When I left Bayside and returned to California, the mysteries followed me. I couldn't outrun them. And through the years, they've stayed with me, wherever I go. They still haven't left.

We used to believe that it was something about Bay-side—that all the mysteries originated there. In time, though, I realized that we were the true avatars of the mysteries. The mysteries were within us.

How long ago had the mysteries chosen us—why did they pick us and let others go free?

Why did they remain inside of us, making our bodies into caves of secrets, places so dark and strange we needed maps to navigate, dead mystery-filled places we couldn't run from or escape—we never could—making us long for a time when there would be no more secret places in the world.

At Tommy Tomorrow's funeral years ago in Star City, his brother placed a gold coin underneath his tongue. It was a custom, I understood, a coin for the dead to be able to pay for passage to cross the river. But I remembered thinking then, confused with grief, would it be that river in Hades that Tommy was expected to cross? It didn't make any sense, for a boy detective to be sent down to hell, and I tried futilely to stop thinking of customs and rituals that were not my own. Egyptians buried their kings in pyramids filled with gold, I knew. Tomb raiders hoped to be the first to open a royal tomb to find it as it was the day the mourners left and the entrance was sealed. They yearned to be the lucky ones to disturb the peace of a dead king. Along with their riches, Egyptian kings were buried with canopic jars holding their internal organs, with their favorite personal possessions, and with *shabtis*—miniature human figures representing servants and assistants to accompany them into the afterlife. The burial pyramid of Thatmose I, a king of the Twenty-first Dynasty, offers an enduring mystery. When the pyramid was disturbed, wrapped in the bandages which should have held a fifty-year-old king were the remains of an unknown boy of eighteen. I wondered: Who was this boy, who found himself sealed in that burial chamber? All those years, was he waiting for discovery, for his future to find and unbury him? Would he open his eyes, only pretending to be asleep and impersonating a dead king, and then would he rise up to greet a new life? What was that boy thinking, lying there, waiting for the future to discover him and the secrets he held in silence for hundreds of years.

Inside the pyramid of Tutankhamen, archeologists discovered the coffins of two little girls next to the blackened and shrunken remains of the dead king. This was another mystery from the New Kingdom. Were they his daughters, who both mysteriously died young? Were they sacrificed upon the death of their father, to join him for all eternity? Or were they two girl sleuths who wandered into the story and never found their way out? In *The Mystery of the Gold Coins* four of us boy detectives—Joe, Josh, Rex, and me—almost found out what it would be like to spend all eternity that way. Our investigation led us to Glenn Michaels, a psycho gold smuggler obsessed with Egyptian artifacts who drugged and captured us. When we awoke we were in a dark chamber. The air was hot, and we were stripped down to white briefs and chained, a fetishist's wet dream. Our hands were bound behind us. It was as steamy and foggy as a sauna, and in the dark and mist I could faintly see gold statues of strange animals and humans surrounding us. I was sweating and hallucinating. Michaels said he was going to encase us all in gold— we would be golden boys literally, stuck forever in the moment of our bright youth. Torpedo, Rex's chimpanzee, saved us, stealing the keys to unlock our manacles and helping us make our escape. It wasn't a pyramid we were locked inside, after all, like that sick fuck Michaels said—it was really his basement, and he didn't even have enough gold to cover all four of us. I must admit I've wondered what it would have been like to be frozen solid in that moment, to become so hard as to be able to endure the years and be found centuries later, like the children in those pyramids, and to have the people of the future wonder: *Who are these boys? How did they get here? What mystery happened to them so many years ago?*

In the Henry Darger paintings that depict the great long war fought by the Vivian Girls and their allies against the military of their opposition, enemy soldiers hide in the battlefield disguised as statues. The war makes them so hard they resemble stone. The soldiers stand perfectly still, impersonating the non-living, then surprise the Vivian Girls who wander into the scene unawares as the statues come alive to strangle them.

In a boxed set retrospective, a veteran artist says of a defining song from his early years that he stole the title from an old movie and borrowed the vocal style from Roy Orbison, but *the innocence at the time was mine.*

Back in our youth we would have been the innocents, so naive as to be fooled by men hiding in plain view as statues. Today, I'm afraid, we'd be more like the statues, grown so hard as to be able to resemble stone.

During the mysteries, we tried hard not to cry but sometimes it happened. I almost lost it when we were tied up as hostages during *The Secret of the Chinese Boat,* and when we were captured by Glenn Michaels in *The Mystery of the Gold Coins* Joe started sobbing uncontrollably, the tears falling and his hands tied back, unable to hide or wipe them. He was right next to me, but my hands were behind me as well and I was gagged, so there was nothing I could do or say. I knew that when we cried it wasn't necessarily for the moment at hand, but for other things that moment made us remember. As Joe wept, Michaels got annoyed, Joe's sobs a distraction to his psycho ranting. He yelled, *Hey, kid—what's your fucking damage?!* and kicked Joe hard in the mouth.

The children buried in the tombs were like child saints—they all died young. Years ago I could have been a saint, too, but then the years happened. If child saints and those children preserved in bandages had lived longer, time would have turned them hard as well, I think. How many more years would they have had to live before they, too, would be able to name their fucking damage? How long before they would know more than they'd want to about the secrets of the world around them? How long before they'd discover the lessons we were taught as sleuths: In time you learn to assess your damages and move on, learn to be awesome in your ways of survival, and learn to not fear trouble until it comes.

Today, when I recall *The Secret of the Chinese Boat*, what stays with me is not the convoluted events or the resolution of that case but the physical sensations that so many years later remain vivid. I still remember the rocking of the boat as we were lost at sea, and the smell of the ocean, and the taste of blood in my mouth, and, of course, the shock of lightning. When I think of that case I still feel the ropes around my wrists.

We had to jump from our captors' boat that way, escaping into the ocean, into that undersea world where we longed to remain, letting all that water wash away the hurt.

It was my first big case, and when I recall that mystery, it's always remembered with my hands bound behind me. It's sad, but that was how the boy detective life was. During this one case, the list of crap that happened to us boy sleuths was incredible:

- We had our boat sabotaged, and we nearly sank into the ocean;
- We were constantly threatened, verbally and physically, by a number of strange men;
- We were held hostage, gagged, our hands bound, aboard our captors' boat;
- To escape the above, we jumped, still bound together, into the icy waters of Bayside Bay, where we nearly drowned;
- Frank, Joe, and the others were attacked by men on the pier;
- As the attack occurred, I was struck by lightning;
- Chet nearly drowned twice, granted once out of his own stupidity, but the second time when he was tossed overboard by bad guys wanting to take our boat, the *Golden Promise*;
- While searching through an underground cave at the end of the mystery, we had to flee for our lives from a cave-in.

There's more I'm forgetting, but we survived it. We survived it all to live another day. After that mystery ended, I remember stumbling home to my grandparents' house. I had seen the lone searchlight from the western cliffs and was still high from that. I had been staying at Frank and Joe's house while the case was ongoing, and I carried home a backpack of my stuff—clothes and things. I snuck into my room and emptied out the backpack before going to sleep. I took out the certificates for my shares of rare blue amber and put them in my writing journal. I unpacked my toiletries and neatly folded the clothes that were still wearable and put them all away. I took out my tools of the trade—my magnifying glass, my fingerprinting kit, my surveillance binoculars, my hand-held tape recorder, and my detective's notebook—and I hid them. Finally, I reached down to the bottom of the bag and took out the clothes that were soaked in blood. It was not all my own blood, either. Some was Joe's, and some of it was from the other guys on the case. I wrapped the clothes in layers of plastic supermarket bags, and I hid the bundle in the corner of the closet.

When I left Bayside at the end of that summer, I took that bundle back to California, and I've kept those unwashed clothes ever since. When I went away to college, I carried that bundle with me as a reminder of my first true mystery. For four years, that pile of clothes traveled with me from dorm rooms to apartments, all that remained of the *Chinese Boat* mystery besides my memory of it.

What else survives the mysteries?

To get through cases, we had to sacrifice parts of ourselves—there was no way to remain whole. Barters were made. A hand extended during a fall saves the body. A bloody palm becomes a sacrifice, taking the place of a broken arm; a knee is scraped raw in place of a concussion; broken ribs were exchanged for broken spines. Clothing became bloodied and torn and ruined.

In time, we learned to sew. We learned to stitch together what we could repair and save. We learned to survive our lives, always chased, always running, splashing through mud and rain, running through cornfields and wheat fields and caves and forests, tripping over vines and rocks and holes and each other in our efforts to stay alive, falling, stumbling, bloodied and tired, our feet hurting from the distance we fled.

And always, we asked ourselves: What was lost? What was left of us, after all the battering? Living through the mysteries, what can possibly survive?

What remains?

In the *Aliens* movies, there are moments known as *the backward glance*. It is the moment when a character, running away from one of the title creatures, unknowingly signals their own doom. They dare to look back. Those who perform the backward glance are always the next to die. In seconds, they will be snacks for the aliens. Their death is destined, foretold by their mistake, by having made the fatal error of not looking ahead.

As boy and girl detectives, we too were meant to look forward and never look back. We were supposed to always live for the future, never reflecting, all eyes ahead as we'd be hit with the next mystery, and then the next. To look back was to risk being frozen in time or frozen in stone; smart sleuths marched straight ahead, eyes forward, like good soldiers of the mysteries, expressing no regrets.

But I've found that to never look back is also to never

understand or learn. It is to be frozen in perpetual un-awareness. And I've come to realize that this, too, in it's own way, is a worse kind of turning to stone.

I feel like I've said this before elsewhere, that it's what I've been trying to say all along. I've been thinking about it for so damn long, but in the end it's the whole point of what I'm doing in asking these questions about our lives.

Sometimes, I feel like I'm finally getting somewhere, making some progress in understanding the way we lived. And sometimes, when I'm overwhelmed by all the thinking and the questions, I feel like I've become a victim of the glance backward, that I've now marked my fate by daring to try to understand and explain and record all that happened. I may have doomed my-self—I may have unwittingly turned myself to stone, with any hope for happiness and contentment now gone to bone. I may have engineered my own post-modern mystery, the kind where the criminal and the victim are one and the same, and there's no true end-ing, only more questions.

Back there in Bayside, we detectives made faustian bar-gains with the mysteries. We traded bright-eyed youth and beauty for knowledge. We exchanged innocence for the heart of the story. We bartered ordinary lives for lives wrapped in intrigue. Grown up, we live with those decisions made in weakness and in youth, now able to weigh with hindsight all that it cost us. What could we keep of ourselves—fighting to survive, saving each other when we could, trying not to let it devour us when we couldn't, always on the edge of a terrible mystery that we tried to enter boldly?

What could bring us all back alive?

I'm sitting here in New York, watching the first snow-fall of the season—the first of the new millennium—and thinking about all of this. I'm thinking about how this might help us, right here and right now. In the background the horrible vice president of the office where I'm working who we all call Devil-Rob is pacing the hallways, and I'm trying to look busy while stealing time trying to think this through. Through the window I watch snow falling on the Empire State Building; it'll be lighted red and yellow tonight to mark the Chinese New Year. A row of stone lions perched on the rooftop of the hotel across the street—lions, not gargoyles, though they could be gryphons—have all grown white eyebrows of snow while on guard. The neon sign from Jack's 99¢ Store flashes like a beacon, sending out mysterious signals. The spire of the Chrysler Building is covered in fog and snow. I know it doesn't mean anything—the flashing neon sign, the color of the Empire State Building, the hidden spire, the patiently-waiting lions—all are innocent and not the portent of a new mystery. There's nothing hidden there, and there doesn't have to be, and I'm glad for it. These buildings are here, and they've been standing throughout all those years before I ever came to New York, when I was still lost in the mysteries in Bayside and California. They are here, and so am I. All this stands, years after the adventures have ended. All this remains.

OPEN CIRCLES

1

When I was young, China was a place I entered in daydreams, where people walking in the streets and cities looked like my family. I imagined white mountains and tigers that spoke to little boys, every Chinese evening with a full moon and a moonlady who rose up with it, smiling into the vast night. China was created in my mind from American movies and books. There barbers gave boys good luck haircuts the day before they left for America, a place where gold coins would pave the streets. I envisioned how things in China were so different from my life in Los Angeles, how snow fell in winter. I pictured big snowflakes like the ones we cut out of colored tissue paper in school falling through the air, imagined the sounds of crunching as people walked through roads full of snowflakes laid out like a blanket of colors.

And then I thought: if it was so great, why did we ever leave?

• • •

When my grandmother passed away, my father went to Chicago to help my grandfather with the funeral arrangements. Although we stayed with these grand-parents for two years when we first came to the U.S., I was too young then to have any recollection of them. What I know I've gathered from faded photographs, and from the mementos of their lives that were passed down to my father after they died. My grandfather's war medals, his old Webster's Dictionary with cigarette burns scarring the pages, and his gold cuff links are all that I have to form a portrait of the grandfather who came to America before my own father did, later send-ing for his wife but leaving his by-then grown children in China.

He passed on five years after my grandmother, who died when I was six. My father brought back very few of her things, because my grandfather insisted on keeping her clothes and valuables on the farm where he would live for five more years, spending time alone with his memories of her. My father did bring back a jar of fire-flies, to show me a bit of how things were at my grand-parents' farm during the two years I don't remember living there. With the door of the closet shut, I stared at the fireflies for hours until the little lights flickered off, one by one.

What my father couldn't bring back, even though I asked him to, was snow. In Los Angeles we didn't have snow, of course, and I knew of it only from movies and from the stories my brother Bobby told of sledding on the hillside groves of our grandparents' farm. My father didn't tell me he couldn't bring back snow—he rarely took the time to explain things. I found out when he came back empty-handed, and when Bobby explained it to me while he was gone.

—Why won't he bring any back? I asked Bobby.

—He can't, Bobby explained. —Snow melts into water. It never lasts forever.

China, the land we had left, was the exact opposite of where we lived now, I believed. As a child I decided that when it snowed in China, America had no snow, and when it snowed in America, clear skies covered China. I deduced this from playing for hours with a dime-store paperweight, which had two small towns encaged in glass and fake, glittery snow that fell between them. The cities were on either ends of the hourglass structure, located on opposite sides of the glass world, and the snow inside the glass never melted, it only shifted from city to city. When one city was upright, the other stood upside down, the perfect houses within it hanging precariously in the air.

The bottom of the paperweight said MADE IN CHINA, so I assumed one was a Chinese town and the other an American one. The two looked almost exactly alike, and only years later would I realize that both towns were meant to depict Norman Rockwell-like New England hamlets. Turning the paperweight over, snow dropped from one city onto the other, falling slowly through the space in-between before covering the opposite city. A thick blanket of white buried the city completely, blurring the shapes of the houses, the steeples, and the schools, until finally you could only picture from unfaithful memory what was hidden underneath.

2

For years we knew the exact date my brother Bobby left us. It was February 24, a Monday, and the page for that date was left open on his abandoned desk calendar. Not until weeks later, though, did I realize that he wasn't coming back. In the months and years that followed, the calendar page collected dust and yellowed in Bobby's room, a place our mother kept unused. He had left all his clothes, his alarm clock, the things on his desk—everything. The car was still around, so I guess he walked or took the bus. The day before he'd had an intense argument with our parents about not taking his medication like he should, but these often violent clashes had marked the majority of these years living with my older brother, long, seemingly unending years after he changed.

That night was the last time I ever saw him.

Before he changed, Bobby was my hero. Because he was fifteen years older than me, he always acted more like a parent to me than like an older sibling. He was the one who came, for example, to my Christmas concert in kindergarten, walking through the door and easing my anxiety just before I had to stand up and announce that the class would now sing "Jingle Bells." Because our parents couldn't speak English, he was the one who dealt with my schoolteachers when I was young, who took me shopping and to Disneyland. Our father was always working, and our mom also went to work at one of the Chinatown garment factories after I was old enough to attend school, so Bobby did what our parents couldn't. And for a time, things were almost perfect.

Bobby began changing when I was eight. He had had some problems shortly after I was born, and I remember vaguely from my first years of life scenes of family conflicts filled with shouting and violence, dark pieces in my jigsaw puzzle box of memories. Those years are secret ones, never discussed by my parents. Bobby was put away for a while, that I know, and when he came out everyone hoped to forget the crisis. And for a stretch of almost five years, time passed uneventfully, if tensely. It was like dancing in a glass shop, each day a test, successful if nothing happened.

We all somehow knew the day would come when everything would crash to the floor, as if those years were merely time suspended waiting for our lives to break into pieces as sharp as the reality we encountered once Bobby took a turn for the worse.

Behind the locked door of his room we heard violent conversations, knowing he was in there alone. He came out acting as if everything was normal, transforming himself instantly into someone else—the perfect brother I knew before.

But the illusion didn't last. He was fired for his strange behavior from the accounting office where he worked, which made things worse. He had nowhere to go, so he stayed home in his room. At night the arguments with himself grew louder and more violent, lasting hours. At one point he moved out into his own apartment. My parents were hopeful, thinking this might help him, but he returned a month later.

The doctors weren't effective, and eventually he refused to make the visits, refused the medication prescribed to him. —It hurts! he screamed, flushing the pills down the toilet. My parents grew worried that he might kidnap me and run off. They were afraid to leave me alone with him.

Eventually my parents sent him to stay with my grandfather, hoping his influence would stabilize Bobby, but being in the Midwest seemed to make him even crazier. It didn't help that at the time my grandfather himself acted as if people who weren't really there were present, haunted as he was by memories of my recently-departed grandmother. Bobby's talking to the air didn't seem so strange in that farmhouse occupied by ghosts, and soon Bobby came back home, unchanged.

My parents struggled with Bobby's craziness for almost three more years, until that day when he left us in our silent house to wonder and worry about where he went. The house became empty without Bobby, without the sound of his voice. After he was gone I often stayed in his room, listening to the top forty countdown for hours on his clock radio. I went through the letters he wrote in his delusions, about how he was kidnapped from a royal family and was the true heir to a throne; how hired mobsters were after him on the street; how he was unjustly fired because he had discovered secrets in his accounting office.

He never came back.

It took me three years after his departure before I could convince my parents to let me move into his larger room. My father acted like nothing had happened, as if it wasn't all that strange for us to experience such a sudden loss in our lives. My mother carefully packed all his things in boxes before relocating them to the basement, holding out hope that one day Bobby would return home and to his true self. She kept the calendar opened to the Monday that he disappeared, a reminder of the years that had passed by both so quickly and so unbearably slow. Time took on a new dimension in Bobby's absence, like something that we had to go through before that moment when he would return. It was as if normal time had skidded off its rightful track when Bobby left, to be corrected once he arrived safely back home. We held out through the long years, years when the living room clock was never correct, behind ten to twenty minutes each hour in Bobby's absence.

Jogging on the streets of the city, I daydreamed of running into Bobby on the street. Los Angeles is a big city, big enough to swallow someone up and hide him for years and years. I believed that if I extended the boundaries of my run each day, I might one day cross over into his world, meet up with him, and bring him back.

Life after he left was pretty fucked. At times it felt like I was living a half a dozen Afterschool Specials simultaneously. Part of it was just growing up, I realize, but a lot had to do with him. Things kind of evened out by the time I got to high school, although we never found out where Bobby went or what became of him. His absence continued to haunt our house; sometimes I thought it would be better if we at least knew he was dead, so that we could bury our hopes and sleep through the nights without him shadowing our dreams.

With him gone, I missed out on a lot of things he could've helped me with. My parents weren't much help—too Chinese, and too shattered by his disappearance. I never learned to drive, something Bobby promised he would teach me to do when as a kid he let me sit in his lap and steer on the highway. I was lucky my friend Matthew had a car and drove me places. While Matt drove, I'd stare out the window and remember the sights that Bobby always pointed out to me as a kid— the giant neon pie in front of the Palace of Pies restaurant in Los Feliz, the Hollywood sign that glowed a heavenly white up in the hills at night, the giant Bullwinkle statue on Melrose dressed as a rugby player for What's-a-Matter University. My memories of these places were inseparable from my memory of Bobby.

Every time we drove past part of the empty L.A. River—past the graffiti-covered concrete, past the litter blanketing the ground—I made a mental note of the round steel disks oddly dotting the walls, jutting out a few feet. I've never figured out what they are—the openings to valves, or merely an architectural design, or a secret infrastructure leading into the heart of a river that has stopped flowing. An artist painted cat faces on all these disks, smiling, yawning, and sleeping felines whom Bobby would imitate with a purr as we passed by, years ago. He promised that one day I could get a cat— I would name her Sasquatch, I declared.

Seeing our feline friends from so long ago, their faces now peeling with age, I'd wonder what ever became of Bobby—or, for that matter, the young boy who was once so easily pleased with noises and empty promises. The almond-shaped eyes always stared back, silent as Bobby's empty room, amid the sounds of traffic over-powering any ghostly echoes of a river which years past flowed strongly, freely, carrying water out through the city.

I dreamt of leaving, like Bobby did, but I had no place to go. When Matt and I projected our lives into the future, I was blind. I could never see myself ten years ahead, in an age full of possibilities.

I was too tied down to the present, grounded in the here and now. Matt, on the other hand, had his life planned ahead of him. A cellist who had studied under the most renowned master teachers, he would travel to Europe after high school, working with the best instruc-tors in Sweden, Germany, and France before returning to the States to start a successful career. When I first met him, he had already appeared on the *Tonight Show*, an Emmy Awards telecast, and an episode of *That's Incredible* with the other members of his quartet, three Asian American girls given to wearing starched flowery dresses.

On *That's Incredible* they were introduced by Fran Tarkenton as amazing child prodigies, all of them having been weaned on music from birth. Matthew had played the cello since the age of three, starting out on a specially-sized instrument. After a brief taped segment, the four musicians were brought onto the stage before the studio audience where they performed a short piece. The pianist, her shoulders intensely hunched over the keyboard, started the piece with a solo, and Matthew ended it with an arrogant flourish of his bow. As good as they were, the quartet, who dubbed themselves the California Angels, paled in comparison to the other stories on the show.

Those stories explored the unexplainable, the unbelievable—the dark, hidden mysteries coexisting in this world with the normal and mundane. In Montana the walls of a house emit piercing screams regularly, sometimes spilling forth blood; investigations uncover a series of brutal murders of young women occurred there a decade ago. A man falls from a plane and his parachute fails to open; he survives the thousand-foot drop, incurring only minor injuries. Across the country people receive collect calls from the dead; once connected, the long absent deceased have little to say.

Stories like these were the ones viewers tuned in for. They watched for onstage demonstrations of men lying on beds of nails, walking through hot coals, and juggling chainsaws with their teeth.

I'm sure that the viewers, like me, examined the fabric of their own lives against the backdrop of stories of killer bees coming north from Latin America or people born without fingerprints. Stories of cursed artifacts, encounters with extraterrestrials, and celebrity ghosts brought a slice of hope into the ordinariness of simple, everyday lives. Viewers entered a Bermuda Triangle of their own imagination, a secret place where anything was possible: love, fame, and all the returns.

If the possibility existed of life out there in the vastness of space, then surely my brother could return to us, cured and better than before. In a world where great statues are found on remote islands, where herds of cows are mysteriously butchered by laser technology in remote areas of Kansas, and where fighter planes disappear without a trace into thin air, losing sight of all land, the possibilities appeared endless.

In the stories of spontaneous combustion, in the sightings of intangible ghosts and the visions of angels, I found a reason to believe.

Haunted houses were a frequent subject of this show, homes violated by events without explanation. Scientists looking for answers theorized that electromagnetic waves circled the globe, and that in instances of exceeding emotion—a murder or rape or other act of violence, for example—the electromagnetic energy unleashed by a victim could be so strong as to remain for years, soaking into the walls and floors of the site. The energy remains as a witness to the act, to tell again and again that which cannot be forgotten. The terror is shared, repeated, perhaps so that the pain may be in some way lessened.

The California of my growing up was a haunted time, when the pain resonated so thoroughly some days as to seem unbearable. The ghost of my brother would appear momentarily in strangers on the street bearing a slight resemblance, a twitch or gesture that reminded me of Bobby. The history of his life intersected time and time again with my present, my future. The ghost of his illness kept me awake nights, afraid of going to sleep and waking up as insane as he was, changing overnight into some out-of-control lunatic.

Madness formed the backdrop to a life under smog and the buzzing overhead of airplanes flying off to distant places I would never see. When my friends experimented with liquor and drugs I never indulged, afraid of that one drink or snort that would take me over the edge. I didn't particularly want to see that other side, the world Jim Morrison entreated us to break on through to from speakers in living rooms hazy with pot smoke. The history of the sixties stepped forward to meet the present when I was in high school, where the son of Abbie Hoffman was among my classmates. Paisley shirts and round little Lennon glasses came back into vogue, were cool, but the dark spectres haunting that age also came forth, waiting for us down the block.

Matthew lived on Waverly Drive, two blocks away from our high school and one block down from the house that Charles Manson made famous. It was said that during that year their parents were murdered in their home a few blocks away, the LaBianca children were students at the high school. In the aftermath, however, the neighborhood managed to escape the stigma of the past. It was prime Los Angeles realty, after all, and property prices managed to stay competitive even after the killings. Glancing down the street every time I visited Matthew, I saw a simple home, someone's dream house. The grass was neatly trimmed, there was the ubiquitous armed response security sign that every home on the block had, and a picket fence circled the yard, an arc of pure whiteness. The image was perfect.

It reminded me of the picture-perfectness of the high school, which many years earlier served as the film site for the school scenes in *Rebel Without a Cause*. On this campus James Dean and Natalie Wood played confused teens assuming a series of poses, trying to find one that fit. Since those days the school served again and again as a location for many other movies and television shows, Hollywood seduced by the stunning red brick exterior of the campus's main building. When the big earthquake of 1971 destroyed the school's equally picturesque cafeteria and dangerously weakened the central building's structure, this red brick facade was scheduled for demolition. But despite the threat of it collapsing with the next quake, community activists, screenwriters, architects, and other admirers declared the building much too beautiful and important to be destroyed, and saved it by having it named an official L.A. landmark.

The school's exterior suggested the typical American high school, and directors brought in picture-perfect teen actors to portray Hollywood's vision of all-American high school life, one which sharply contradicted the lives of the students who watched from the sidelines as the lives they should have led were filmed before their eyes. Private security crews were needed to protect the movie people from the actual students, and like the buildings of the school itself, the scripted illusions of carefree, happy youth always threatened to collapse at any moment.

Here in this place I constantly stumbled, crossing boundaries and assuming a variety of roles as unreal as any Hollywood movie. Bobby was my secret past, a hidden shame I concealed like a switchblade in my pocket, like a lie from a lover, like James Dean masking his vulnerability in a cool pose against the backdrop of a Hollywood sky.

The man who cuts my hair found a single red hair growing in my head of black last week. When I look in the mirror I can't help searching for it. I wish Bobby were here for me to share this with, so I could maybe determine whether this is a genetic trait in our family.

But he is not here, and I haven't seen him in more than a decade. For all that I know, he could be working in the oil fields in Alaska, building farms in North Dakota, or buried in an unmarked grave in San Diego. If he is alive, he would be approaching forty now. If I were to walk past him on the street, I wonder if I would recognize him, an older version of myself, or would I not see the changes to come in my own face, the way I will carry my age.

I remember an incident, the first time I feared that he would leave me. He had taken me to Woolworth's and told me he wanted to quickly buy some toothpaste inside, leaving me alone in the foyer of the store and promising to return soon. I was six, and I stood gazing at the brightly-colored magazines in the stacks, moving towards the Marvel comics displayed in the wire stand. I wasn't supposed to touch, I knew, so I just looked at the covers showing all the heroes.

I waited and waited, but Bobby didn't come back for me. I began crying and rushed into the store. I was small enough to squeeze under the turnstile, and I ran through the aisles of medicines and household goods, calling for him. He heard me and came, picking me up. —Didn't I say to wait for me? he demanded, shaking me. He seemed angry. On the drive back home it started to rain. Dark clouds blocked the sun, and raindrops fell down on the windshield creating small running rivers that blurred our vision.

3

My family emigrated to America during my first years of life, leaving an entire country behind. Years later, Bobby would abruptly leave behind an entire life and me, never to be heard from again. In the years following Bobby's departure I made my own plans to leave, quietly waiting for the perfect moment. In the meantime, I was living in Bobby's old room.

He had kept a private phone line in his room which we still maintained, so the phone bills continued to come each month addressed to my missing brother, along with occasional pieces of junk mail. This phone was used only to call out, so when Bobby's phone rang we knew for sure that it wasn't anyone we knew, and probably just someone trying to sell life insurance or magazine subscriptions. About four years after Bobby went missing, however, we began receiving calls during which the caller on the other end said nothing, not a word. After a few seconds, the person would hang up. These calls became regular—every other week, sometimes more frequently, we received another voiceless call. I was always the one who inevitably answered them.

If I strained to listen to the sounds in the background, I sometimes heard traffic, sometimes nothing except the electric buzzing of the wires. The caller never spoke. Once, when this phone rang, I picked it up and didn't say a word, waiting for the caller to speak first. A sharp click was followed by a buzz tone.

I wasn't sure whether it was Bobby, and if so, why he would suddenly begin calling four years after he left. —Hey, Bobby—is that you? I once asked, receiving no response.

The only things of Bobby's that weren't packed up and put away in the basement were his desk calendar and his clock radio, which I still used to listen to Casey Kasem, then later to Rick Dees after he started doing the Top 40 countdown. About three months after the mysterious calls began, I started logging them onto Bobby's desk calendar. I didn't dare touch the page opened to the day he left, so I wrote with a red fine point marker on the days after it. The phone would remain quiet for weeks, then shock me from my sleep or reading or rest with its unexpected ringing. Sometimes the calls came in the middle of the night, shattering the silence in the house until I stumbled out of bed to be greeted with silence. A series of red marker dates began filling the desk calendar pages.

One night I fell into a deep sleep, dreaming. It was summer, and I had left the window open for the night. I had seen the dark clouds in the distance as the sun set earlier that day, but I didn't catch their meaning. In the middle of my dream, it began to storm. The wind blew the shades violently, cracking their edges against the windowsill. I heard this, and the drops of rain blowing through the screen and falling onto the desk, but I couldn't wake from my dream.

I was crossing an ocean on a boat, looking out across the water for a sign of land. My mother was holding me, and all of the passengers were hungry and cold. The ship rocked and rocked, and many fell ill. Big, noisy birds circled overhead. No one thought of what they had left behind—they only thought ahead to their new lives. I don't know whether this was a race memory, or my recollection of my own family's voyage. (But we came over on a *plane*—I was only one and a half years old.) When I awoke in the morning, the rain had stopped.

The desk was wet, water covering the floor. The desk calendar was soaked, but dried after a few hours, the pages turning brittle and wrinkled.

Ink from the fine point marker had soaked into the page on top, smearing red stains all over the date marking Bobby's disappearance like marks of shame.

Some nights I stayed out as long as I could, anything to avoid returning home. The California nights were never too cold, and the RTD buses ran throughout the night, carrying lone passengers whose closed-off faces were seen lit through the windows. One night I was coming back from Westwood and heading to the high school for something or another, waiting for bus number 175. By this time I was involved in a number of activities at the school and taking classes at UCLA as well, assuming the identity of the perfect student. It was a bluff, but that role was an easy one for me to play, and the scholarship student route was the one way I found of leaving, disappearing in a more graceful way than Bobby's sudden departure.

I waited for the bus for over an hour before I decided it was time to move on and I began walking.

Cars passed me, their headlights lighting up the stretch of road. A few blocks ahead golden arches towered in the sky. I stuck out my thumb to hitch a ride. One car stops, a red sportscar, newly-polished. I see my reflection in the windshield, illuminated by the light from the arches: a boy not knowing where he's going, only that he needs to keep going, moving somewhere.

The driver seems safe enough, and his car is nice. As he begins to drive I notice his nervous breathing, can see the up and down rhythms of his chest. He seems like an okay guy, not too attractive, but he owns an expensive car. He closes the windows with the automatic button, turns on the heater, and says to me, —It'll be really warm in here soon, so you can take off your jacket if you want. He shows me how to adjust my seat for more leg room.

—I'm fine, thanks, I say. Midway to the school he stops in front of an abandoned church and asks me if we can sit for a bit. He gives me some story about how he's supposed to meet someone, his nephew. I look at my watch and I think I'm going to be late after all. Then the guy tries to make small talk, and it's his car and I need a ride.

After a few minutes pass and no one has shown up, he stalls for more time. —Can we wait just a while more? he asks. —I guess, I say. I can hear each of his nervous little swallows and his shallow breathing. I turn on the radio, and this is a mistake, because he takes it as a sign that I'm interested. Swallowing again, he summons up his courage: —Um, what kind of jeans are you wearing?

I'm so put off by the lameness of his come on that I can only reply, —Levi 501s.

—Really, they don't look like them. He gets braver. —Can I feel the pockets?

Before I can reply his shaking hands move toward my crotch. As his hands grope for me, I take them and put them back on his side of the car. —I need to go, I say calmly.

—Are you sure you can't wait a little longer? he almost begs.

—No. Let's get moving.

He drives in silence the rest of the way. —Here you are, he smiles, as if nothing had happened. He lets me off across from the school. I don't acknowledge his wave good-bye as he heads down the road, disappearing around the corner. I look back at him with the power I'm beginning to learn to feel, the power of the desired.

I take a breath of the night air, look up at the stars twinkling in the sky, and cross the street. It's almost as if I can feel Bobby somewhere out there.

I wonder if there are angels watching over me. In first grade we folded up shredded paper inside white tissues and made ghosts to hang on the October bulletin board. The Mexican American students thought they were angels, *los angeles*, white robed guardians of the city's uncertain future. In weeks, the tissue ghosts, or angels, had shredded from the wind, blowing open easily like a child's trust with the slightest breeze.

Around the same time that I was making plans to leave Los Angeles forever I found a part-time job in Beverly Hills, cataloging the private library of a recently deceased entertainment lawyer. Going into Beverly Hills each time from where I lived in Los Angeles was like crossing borders, and the houses there were all at least five times as large as ours. The lawyer's two daughters hired me from a job posting at UCLA, and when one of them found out I didn't drive she offered to pick me up on the corner of Sunset outside the Beverly Hills Hotel. I didn't know where this was at first, but it was easy to find. It was that famous hotel with the towering pink walls—Hollywood's own memory palace. Nicknamed the Pink Palace, the hotel was the historical site of numerous deals and sordid scandals. It was rumored that the ghosts of some of cinema's earliest stars haunted the halls of the hotel in a netherworld of double illusions.

I had to take the bus to the hotel and then walk inside to call one of the daughters, who would then come to pick me up. The telephone booths were gold-plated and reminded me of *Dynasty*. Outside limos pulled in bearing celebrities, and I recognized the guitarist of some heavy metal band stepping out of one.

The lawyer's house was inaccessible without a car, nestled up in a hillside neighborhood without any sidewalks. It was located next door to the large estate owned by Sammy Davis, Jr. I spent entire days at the house working on the book collection, writing down in long-hand and then typing up lists of authors, titles, publish-ers, and publication dates. It was the nicest house I'd ever been in, like discovering an enchanted castle in a fairy tale.

Among the stacks of books one day, I found an old yearbook from Bradford High School in Lincoln, Nebraska and looked up the photo of a bright-eyed boy headed for Princeton, the one who would move from small town life to Beverly Hills. The lawyer, Mr. Levy, had passed away three months earlier.

A French cook, Marie, made me lunch in the after-noons. She prepared sandwiches thick with gourmet cheese, and the daughters would join me. Both were unmarried and in their thirties; Laureen was a teacher, and Liz drove a Federal Express truck. Privately, Marie confided to me that she was worried about the two of them handling the estate alone: —They have no sense at all. What are they going to do if they don't sell the house before I return to France? Marie's mother had taken ill abroad, and it had been Marie who arranged all the showings of the property, who berated the agent for wasting time bringing over unserious buyers. While I was there Whitney Houston came to look at the house, but she wasn't interested.

Over lunch Marie kept up the conversation with an endless stream of stories. Most of them had to do with "Mister," as she called Mr. Levy. —Never sick before a

day in his life. He became not well, and then, the next
day—Mister gone.

That was why she wanted to see about her mother,
while there was still time. She forced cookies on me,
cookies Mister liked that she still baked from habit. The
tins were full and I was the only one who would eat
them, dunking them in my coffee, which I had to take
black. There was no cream in the house for coffee, only
CoffeeMate.

—Look, I still buy—I don't use, was Mister. But you
get used to—yes, you get used to.

Like the ghost of my grandmother with my grandfather, and like Bobby with myself, it felt then like the
memory of Mister would haunt that house forever, that
life in there began with him as the center and everything else originated from that core even after his
absence. I watched Laureen and Liz stare into their
cups, as the white swirl formed by the cream substitute
spread out in their coffee like an expanding galaxy.

Eventually they did manage to sell the house, and Liz
sent me a pop-up card to congratulate me when I got
into the same college her father had attended. I received it the summer before I left for Princeton, when I
was working as a temp at a terrible office job downtown. By the end of that summer I kept a handmade
calendar next to my desk at work, marking off each
long day until I was free. At the end of the summer I
left knowing I would never go back, walking out across

the street towards the Bonaventure Tower looming overhead. The wind blew perfect cumulus clouds across a deep blue sky, and it was a truly beautiful day. The perfection of the scene was reflected on the black glass of the Tower, where clouds rolled by like a scene shown on a giant movie screen.

During those frustrating years when I wanted to escape, I always read stories and saw movies about teenagers in the Midwest taking buses out to Los Angeles, running away from their small towns to live out their dreams. They were able to lose themselves inside the Hollywood legends of runaways, which I never could. When you live in Los Angeles, there is nowhere to run away to.

Bobby never came back, and the calls remained unexplained, another unsolved mystery.

And after leaving for college, I realized that, all in all, leaving home in 20th century America is such a disappointment. There are no more big locomotives billowing thick black smoke clouds to take you across the country on a journey you will always remember and might one day write about. There are no boats sailing from harbors for distant, unseen American shores—for the Gold Mountain. There are no mythic walks to the jetty. You just get on a plane or a bus—there's one leaving somewhere every half hour—and you go.

In the last semester of high school when grades no longer mattered, I ditched classes often, jumping on RTD buses and riding to the end of the line. Peering out the window on these trips, I kept a lookout for people on the street who resembled Bobby.

Line 242 was a particularly good bus, because the ride lasted for over two hours before ending at its last stop in front of a Mrs. Fields, where I would buy oatmeal raisin cookies and hot cocoa before crossing the street to take the ride back. The route snaked through Chinatown, where I hadn't set foot in years. I remembered vanilla soft freeze cones and orange whip drinks, and throwing up near the wishing pond presided over by the bald Buddha statue. Bobby took me home that day.

Midway in its run one afternoon, about five minutes after leaving Chinatown, the bus passed through an area of railroad tracks, built years before by laborers sweating under a hot American sun. When the crossing light flashed red, the bus stopped in front of the tracks, the roar of engines approaching in the distance. Soon a train passed by, followed by endlessly-linked cargo vessels. The names of long-bankrupt companies appeared on the cargo box sides in worn paint, passing before me like a parade of apocrypha. The boxcars spoke of better, simpler days, a time when rails stretched across the entire nation. Now, most of the vessels held nothing, the few full ones carrying animals going to slaughter, cattle with swishing tails who stared vacantly back at me through the slate boards with blinking eyes.

Acknowledgments

I owe an enormous gratitude to the teachers who took the time to read early versions of these stories— Thomas Keneally, Stuart Dybek, John Calvin Batchelor, Gabriele Schwab, Peter Bacho, Reginald McKnight, Wayne Fields, Benjamin Taylor, Donald Faulkner, and Maureen Howard. Their faith and care is reflected in the preceding pages.

Thanks to everyone who offered encouragement and support—thanks especially to Wey-Wey Kwok, who read these stories from the very beginning. In California, where most of these stories were born, thanks to—Homer Brown, who discussed film *noir* with me; Isabelle Dore, who bought me lunch when I was broke; Howard Elinson; Marion Erling; James Maynard; Frank Nguyen, Walter Kiang, and Christine Truong; the Rosten family in Balboa (including Puccini, who accompanied me on walks along the ocean as I dreamt of moving to New York); Bea Tran; and Andrea Wyser-

Orpineda and family. In New York—thanks to the editors at the magazines that published earlier versions of these stories; thanks to Chris Featherman; thanks to Blue for the bootleg MSWord; for kind professional counsel at crucial times thanks to Jenny Bent, Bill Clegg, Warren Frazier, Jonathan Galassi, Eric Simonoff, and Sandra Zane; thanks to all the members of Team Context, including Trevor Bundy, Carol Devine Carson, Nick Einenkel, and Cassandra Pappas; thanks to Kiki Smith for the use of her beautiful art.

Special thanks to the late Mr. Donald A. Strauss and the late Mrs. Dorothy Strauss for generous financial support in the form of a fellowship which provided time to work on this book, and whose good works continue on with the Strauss Foundation. I will never forget the early encouragement and belief in this book by the late Robert Jones, who I regret I never had the chance to meet in person and thank for his kindness as an editor and a writer.

Finally, my gratitude and debt to the goblin king of this book, Beau Friedlander, for not giving up on me and for letting these stories be read—this book would not exist without him.